An Unlikely Duet

Lelia M. Silver

The characters and events portrayed in this book are fictitious or are used fictitiously. Any similarity to real persons, living or dead, is purely coincidental and not intended by the author.

ISBN: 1479164852
ISBN-13: 978-1479164851

LCC

To Heather-

I promise you don't have to check every page of this one.

ACKNOWLEDGMENTS

This book would never have gotten this far without the support and encouragement of my husband and several dear friends and family members. My deepest thanks to all of you. I also must acknowledge the brilliance of Jane Austen. Her characters, plots, and settings are unparalleled. Anything that appears familiar within these pages can be attributed to her.

Pemberley was now Georgiana's home; and the attachment of the sisters was exactly what Darcy had hoped to see. They were able to love each other, even as well as they intended. Georgiana had the highest opinion in the world of Elizabeth; though at first she often listened with an astonishment bordering on alarm at her lively, sportive manner of talking to her brother. He, who had always inspired in herself a respect which almost overcame her affection, she now saw the object of open pleasantry. Her mind received knowledge which had never before fallen in her way. By Elizabeth's instructions she began to comprehend that a woman may take liberties with her husband, which a brother will not allow in a sister more than ten years younger than himself. –Pride and Prejudice

Prologue

I do not claim the talent of being able to converse easily with strangers. I do not have the easy wit and vivacity that my sister does. I cannot claim the attention of the room with a glance or gain the admiration of many with a comment. If I did, perhaps my emergence among the ton would not be so taxing. As it is, I would much rather spend my days here at Pemberley, among my family, than in the finest ballrooms of London. Perhaps if society could see me here, with those I love, they would not judge me so harshly.

Georgiana Darcy looked up from her journal as the sounds of laughter filtered through the open window. Rising from her desk, she moved to stand at the window, looking down at the gardens below. With a content smile, she watched as her brother frolicked on the lawn with his 4 year-old daughter, while Elizabeth looked on from her seat nearby, holding a sleeping, 8 month-old William Darcy. The five years since his marriage had seen Fitzwilliam Darcy become a different man than he once was.

Although Georgiana had always known her brother to be a caring, warm individual, he had blossomed into an openly affectionate man. Where he had once been somber and taciturn, he was now rarely without a smile on his face. Elizabeth had been good for him, as she had been for Georgiana.

Georgiana smiled as she remembered how Elizabeth had drawn her out, boosting her confidence with the local society and then making her laugh at the ridiculousness of the ton during her first season in London. Of course, even having Elizabeth and Fitzwilliam at her side had not made that first season, or any of the subsequent ones, easy. While she had been touted as one of the beauties of that first season, and her wealth had drawn several suitors, her shyness had led many to proclaim her to be proud and aloof. Among those who hadn't been put off by her closed demeanor, most had been fortune hunters or rakes. None had managed to make it past her uneasiness among company to see the real woman underneath.

So, here she was, still unmarried at almost twenty-two, dreading the whispers and giggles that another season would bring. But that was still months away, and so Georgiana determinedly turned her thoughts back to the pleasant scene outside her window.

Returning to her desk, she closed the journal on the disconsolate thoughts it held, and went to join her brother and his wife in the gardens below.

Chapter 1

Elizabeth Darcy smiled at Georgiana as she settled into the chair the servants had placed next to her. "I see you've finally decided to join us. I'm amazed you were able to concentrate on your correspondence with all the noise your brother and Thea are making!"

Georgiana smiled back. "It did make it a little difficult, but once I was finished I couldn't resist the chance to be a part of all the laughter." She gestured to the sleeping baby on her sister's lap. "I am surprised that little William here was able to sleep through it all!"

Elizabeth laughed. "He always has been able to sleep through anything!" She glanced up as her husband approached them, carrying a grinning Thea on his shoulders. "Your brother received a letter from Mr. Bingley this morning. I suspect he's decided that there is no time like the present to share its contents with you."

Darcy settled himself on a nearby bench, handing off his daughter to the waiting nurse. He grinned wryly at his wife. "You are indeed correct, my dear, although I'm shocked I was able to make out any of the message Bingley was trying to convey."

Having seen a few of Bingley's mangled missives, Georgiana and Elizabeth shared a smile.

"Thankfully, I also received a letter from Jane this morning that clarified a few of the points Charles was trying to make," Elizabeth added. "They have invited us to come visit them for a few weeks at Chetborn."

"Apparently Jane is missing her sister terribly and requires her presence," Darcy teased. Sobering, he continued, "However, and this may affect our decision to accept or not, Caroline Crosby and her husband will also be visiting during that time frame."

He looked at his wife. "I realize you and Caroline have not always been on the best of terms, but I know you, too, have been missing your sister. The real question is: are we willing to put up with her company in order to be able to enjoy the Bingleys'? Her husband, Mr. Crosby, really isn't a bad sort of chap. He may have only married her for her money and to have a trophy on his arm, but he's an intelligent man, who cares for his tenants. I believe I would enjoy the chance to get to know him better. But in the end, I would never want you to feel uncomfortable, my dear."

Elizabeth leaned back in her seat and gently rubbed her son's back as he started to stir on her lap. She pondered her husband's words for a few moments, and then spoke decidedly, "I think I can handle Caroline in exchange for the chance to see Jane again. It has been far too long." She turned her attention to Georgiana. "What do you think, dear? Would you be terribly uncomfortable if Caroline were to be in attendance?"

Georgiana hesitated, remembering a few of her run-ins with the legendary Caroline Bingley, and a few of the stories Elizabeth had shared with her. "I would never want to separate Elizabeth from her sister." She glanced at her brother. "And as most of Caroline's scorn is directed toward Elizabeth, and not toward me, I cannot say that I am opposed to the idea of a visit. In fact, I believe I would enjoy seeing little Geoffrey again."

Elizabeth and Darcy both smiled at the thought of their precocious nephew. He was going to give Charles and Jane a run for their money, especially as they tended to dote upon their only child. Being not a little spoilt, and entirely too adorable for his own good, he had the entire household wrapped around his little finger.

"Jane's letter mentioned that he had been up to some mischief," Elizabeth said. "Apparently, something involving a missing feather duster and a bust of Charles' late father. It has been rather bad of me to leave her for so long. You know neither she nor Charles have the disposition to guide young Geoffrey. They are entirely too kind and laid-back for their own well-being."

Elizabeth glanced down at the quiet baby on her lap, who was trying unsuccessfully to cram his toes into his mouth, and laughed before continuing ruefully, "I always thought we would be the ones with the wild, uncontrollable children, while Jane and Charles' children would be well-mannered and orderly. I dare say had they known what was in store they might not have wanted children at all!"

The three adults shared a laugh, but Elizabeth's smile was tinged with sadness. Unlike the others, she knew that while Jane loved the son she did have, she desperately wished for another child. When Jane and Charles had visited after young Will had been born, Jane had stared longingly at the baby. When her sister pressed her, she admitted that she and Charles had been trying unsuccessfully to have another child. Elizabeth hoped that this visit wouldn't be a painful reminder to Jane of what she didn't have.

She turned her attention back to her husband as he rose.

He stretched, and then said, "I'll write to Charles and let him know when to expect us. Would one week from today be sufficient for all your preparations?"

Elizabeth nodded. "That should give me enough time to talk to Mrs. Reynolds and get everything together for the children."

Darcy turned to his sister. "Will that work for you as well, Georgiana?"

Georgiana tilted her head and answered with a smile, "As my affairs are much less difficult to arrange than Elizabeth's, I'd say that a week will be more than sufficient."

Darcy rubbed his hands together, pleased. "Excellent." He bent over to kiss his wife's cheek, and then continued, "Now, I have some business with my steward that I've been neglecting this morning, so I will leave you ladies to your own devices. I probably won't be able to wrap this up before supper, so don't expect me for tea."

With that, he strode off toward the house. Georgiana tilted her head back, basking in the warmth of the sun's rays on her face.

"You know what your Aunt Catherine would say about sitting out here in the sun like that," Elizabeth teased.

Georgiana smiled, and without opening her eyes replied, "You should know by now that I've never had any interest in my Aunt's opinions, as free with them as she is. I'd much rather enjoy the warmth of the sun with those I love than sit in a dreary drawing room by myself."

She opened her eyes and grinned mischievously. "I daresay if Aunt Catherine would take *my* advice on the subject she would be a much happier person." She continued with feigned sorrow, "But, alas, she insists on holing herself away with that dreadful parson of hers."

Elizabeth's eyes twinkled. "Ah, but don't forget that she is doing the rest of us a favor by keeping my cousin occupied. Without Lady Catherine, I have no doubt that he would be accosting us quite regularly with his presence, seeing as how my husband is the illustrious Mr. Darcy of Pemberley."

Georgiana giggled as she pictured the ridiculous Mr. Collins following around her tall, dignified brother, extolling his many virtues. "I suppose then we'll have to thank my aunt for her self-sacrificing spirit. I don't imagine Fitzwilliam would remain civil long under his constant attentions."

Elizabeth shook her head. "No, I don't think he would, although your dear brother would try, for my sake. Frankly, I think we all would be avoiding him. The only one who could stand him would be little William here, and only then because he could sleep through anything!" She sighed. "I do wish there were some way I could see my dear Charlotte again without the inconvenience of having to also see Mr. Collins and Lady Catherine!"

Georgiana patted her comfortingly on the shoulder, and then resumed her previous position, closing her eyes against the sun. "I suppose you will just have to be content with your spinster of a sister for company." She peeked out from beneath her lashes and said wickedly, "Or you can always seek out Caroline Crosby for company. I'm sure she would love to be known as one of your dearest confidantes."

Elizabeth snorted. "Yes, I'm sure she would love to be able to spread gossip about me among the ton, while using my position to climb up the social ladder." She looked over at her sister-in-law and smiled. "No, I find I am quite content with your company, my dear Georgiana. I fear Pemberley will not be the same when you've left us to start your own family."

Georgiana smiled ruefully. "Well, I don't think that you need to fear that will happen anytime soon. I have yet to find any man that could tempt me to leave the comfortable situation I have here at Pemberley. I'm beginning to think there isn't one who exists."

Elizabeth leaned over and patted her arm. "I know you will find the right man someday. I never thought I would end up married at all, much less to the illustrious Mr. Darcy. Love has a funny sense of timing. It likes to sneak up on you when you are least expecting it and hit you over the head. Just be patient and wait for the right man to come along. I want you to have the love and respect in your marriage that your brother and I have. I would have you settle for nothing less."

Georgiana caught Elizabeth's hand as she pulled it away and squeezed it. "Brother and you have quite spoiled me for the marriage market. After seeing the joy in your marriage, I could not possibly settle for anything less."

Elizabeth squeezed her hand back and changed the subject, "Did you hear that Mr. Brightmore is selling his estate, Wylington? Apparently, Mrs. Brightmore has always wanted to live in Bath and Mr. Brightmore has finally given in and agreed to purchase a house there."

"I've often heard Mrs. Brightmore speak of longing to move there. I'm not surprised they've finally decided to go. I understand she grew up near the city and has always loved it. Perhaps the hot springs there will be good for Mr. Brightmore's rheumatism. You know the cold winters here have become increasingly difficult for him," Georgiana replied.

Elizabeth nodded. "Yes, and it would be a good place for the young Misses Brightmore to make their introduction into society. I'm sure their parents took that into account as well when making their decision. I will be sad to see them go. I suppose we could not be so fortunate as to have the new owners also be such good neighbors."

"We can only hope we will find them to be half so kind and good-natured," Georgiana agreed. "Do you think it will be on the market for long?"

Elizabeth shrugged. "It is hard to say. We are out of the way here in Derbyshire, so there are many who would hesitate to be so far from society. However, there are quite a few men out there looking to become landowners and step up in society. I guess only time will tell."

"I hope it is a family," Georgiana pondered. "It would be nice to have some young children in the area for Will and Thea to play with as they get older."

"Yes, your brother and you are far too serious. They need someone that will encourage them to be silly, as children ought to be," Elizabeth replied, with a twinkle in her eye.

Georgiana laughed. "I fear you must think my childhood was very dull indeed! But never fear, Sister, I think you have brought out the child in us all!" She stood, and looked around her. "I think I am going to take a turn among the gardens. Would you like to join me?"

Elizabeth stood, moving Will onto her hip. "No, I need to give this one over to his nurse and speak with Mrs. Reynolds about a few things. Will you be back in time for tea?"

Georgiana nodded. "Of course, as long as I don't lose track of time." She smiled wryly. "You know I often do."

Elizabeth agreed, "If you haven't returned before then I will send one of the servants to collect you. Enjoy your walk."

Georgiana bid her farewell and turned to make her way down to the gardens below. She made her way through the elaborate topiaries and rose gardens, past the flowering bushes and the creeping vines, to her favorite place, a small sort of wilderness well past the main gardens. Wildflowers grew rampant and a small bubbling brook coursed its path through the tall grasses.

She grazed her fingers along the flowers as she passed. Bright black-eyed Susans and dainty Queen Anne's lace danced in her wake. Periwinkle chicory stood staunchly along the path, ignoring her presence, while the airy daisies laughed up at her.

A small copse of trees blocked her from the sight of anyone in the house. She sat down at the base of one of the trees, and glancing around to make sure no one was around, took off her stockings and shoes and slid her feet into the refreshing waters of the brook. She leaned her head back against the trunk of the tree and smiled.

Lately, she had been feeling discontent, restless, trapped, and unable to move forward with her life, as much as she longed to. As much as Georgiana enjoyed being with her family, especially since the addition of her niece and nephew, she wanted to have a home of her own. Elizabeth and Fitzwilliam had never made her feel unwelcome at Pemberley, but she knew that she wanted to be the mistress of her own life. She hated this waiting, not knowing what the future held, and wished she could hurry it along somehow. Her discontent had been slowly growing until it haunted her, a constant reminder that she, Georgiana Darcy, was missing out on something in her life.

But here, among the trees, listening to the babble of the brook and the chirping of the crickets, those thoughts receded and she could feel at peace, at least for awhile. She knew it couldn't last; Elizabeth would be sending one of the servants to find her eventually; but for the moment she relaxed and enjoyed her freedom.

Her mind drifted back to the past season, and a frown marred her face. She remembered the whispers and giggles of the young debutantes, just out, as she passed. The words, "Quite on the shelf, you know," "arrogant, no one cares for her," "rich as Croesus, thinks she's so grand," had floated to her ears. They had cut her deeply, and she knew many shared their viewpoint. She had watched as countless young ladies and young gentlemen paired off, and yet no one had sought her out for a second dance.

She knew it was mostly her fault. She was not easy in company and couldn't seem to get past her shyness enough to converse with those she didn't know. She had tried, and practiced, as Elizabeth had once advised her brother, but to no avail. Whenever she entered a room full of people, and felt all their eyes turn upon her, it was all she could do not to run and hide. So she dealt with the attention the same way her brother had before her: she put up a mask and hoped desperately that everyone would forget about her. But, alas, her fortune and pretty face made her unforgettable, and so the whispers had started.

She dreaded the return of another season and the derision it would bring. At least those first few seasons had held the hope of finding love and happiness. Now, she was resigned to the fact that whether or not the future held marriage for her, she would not be finding the love of her life during the season in London.

A slow smile spread across her features. Perhaps, this time Fitzwilliam would not insist upon her traveling to London for the season. If she started to get him used to the idea now, by the time spring rolled around he might be willing to forgo the trip to Town. She knew his preference was for Pemberley anyway, and now that Elizabeth had children she had no desire to be in society.

With renewed purpose, Georgiana pulled her stockings and shoes back on. She felt her hair for any misplaced strands and checked her appearance as best she could in the reflective surface of the stream. Then turning, she made her way with determined strides back to the house.

*****

Elizabeth watched from an upstairs window as Georgiana made her way back. She was concerned about her sister. Georgiana had become more and more withdrawn since their removal to Pemberley at the onset of summer. She had thrown herself into her music, taking comfort in the familiar works of Beethoven and Mozart, and holding her family at an arm's length.

She frowned down at the familiar blonde head as it bobbed among the shrubberies. Georgiana was trying to hide it, but she sensed the restlessness and unease that reverberated from her very being. She didn't know what to do about it. Her words could only bring a limited amount of comfort, as she knew very well.

She watched as Georgiana paused to speak with one of the gardeners. From the proud smile on the man's face, she was no doubt complimenting him on his efforts. Elizabeth shook her head. Even with so much on her mind, her sister still had the graciousness to take an interest in those around her. She smiled sardonically. She knew of many that would not have.

The smile slowly faded from her face and she rested her forehead against the cool glass. It was only natural for Georgiana to want a home and a family of her own. Elizabeth sighed. Only time could provide the family, but perhaps it was time she talked to Fitzwilliam about releasing Georgiana's dowry to her. She was of age, and it would allow her the independence she craved.

Elizabeth turned from the window and found a seat on the settee. Georgiana was nearly back to the house and it wouldn't do to be caught watching her from the window.

Chapter 2

As they had known it would, the week until their departure flew by. Preparations and last minute things that had to be attended to had kept them busy until, finally, they were driving away from Pemberley. The trip was relatively short, and in the span of a long day's travel they had arrived at Chetborn, the Bingleys having given up Netherfield for the relative privacy of Derbyshire long ago. Jane and Charles Bingley were waiting for them outside when the carriage pulled up.

Jane embraced her sister eagerly. "I'm so glad you've come! You can't possibly know how I've been longing to see you."

"I'm sure she has some inclination of the sort, since she has been missing you dreadfully as well," Darcy responded dryly from behind his wife.

Jane giggled and released her sister. "We've so much to catch up on. Letters just aren't the same. Come in and we'll show you to your rooms. Once you've had a chance to change and relax a bit we can visit."

The small party followed them inside and allowed themselves to be ushered to their rooms. The children were sent up to the nursery to join Geoffrey Bingley and they all agreed to meet up again in the sitting room for tea once they were rested.

Elizabeth had barely closed the door behind the string of servants who had brought up her luggage before she heard a knock from the connecting door and her husband poked his head in.

She smiled, and beckoned for him to come in as she undid the strings on her bonnet. He lounged on the bed and watched her from beneath half-hooded eyes as she sat on the edge of the bed and removed her shoes and stockings. She flexed her feet after their long confinement and glanced up at him from beneath her lashes, a mischievous look in her eyes.

"Did you notice what I noticed?" she asked conspiratorially.

"That depends on what you noticed," Darcy teased. "If you mean Bingley preening and about to burst with pride, I certainly did not notice that."

"Well, *I* noticed that Jane is absolutely *glowing*!" Elizabeth asserted. "I think they might have some very good news to share with us this visit."

Darcy tugged her down beside him and she nestled her head against his shoulder while he tenderly wrapped his arm around her.

"I think you might be right," he admitted. "I don't think Geoffrey will be too happy to share the attention of his parents though!"

Elizabeth laughed. "You're probably right." She pushed herself up on her elbow to look him in the face. "You know I'll have to come back when Jane gets close to her confinement, don't you?"

He tightened his arm around her. "I do. I imagine Georgiana wouldn't mind missing the end of the season." He sighed. "She's already dropping hints about not going to Town for the season next year."

"Can you blame her?" Elizabeth yawned, and laid back down. "I know you felt the same way she does at those balls and parties. Perhaps it's time to start letting her make her own decision on the matter."

"You're probably right," he admitted. "We'll talk about it again when it gets closer to time. Why don't you go ahead and rest? I know you're exhausted."

Elizabeth yawned and snuggled closer. "Only if you stay," she murmured sleepily. "I never can sleep without you."

Darcy smiled down at the top of her head and didn't bother to reply. She was already asleep.

*****

A few doors down, Georgiana was lying wide awake on her bed. A certain amount of anxiety had plagued her since hearing that Caroline Crosby, nee Bingley, was in residence along with her husband. While it was true that Caroline focused her attentions, if they could be called that, on Elizabeth, Georgiana had also found herself on the receiving end of some cutting remarks.

She wished she had the gumption and wit Elizabeth had to stand up to Caroline. Caroline's sarcasm and biting tongue didn't seem to bother her. She was able to easily laugh them off.

It was not so easy for Georgiana. She wasn't able to easily dismiss Caroline's words from her thoughts. The lack of respect Caroline displayed towards her cut her to the core. In her company she was often only a shell of herself, afraid to say anything that might bring censure. There was no way of knowing what would bring the biting remarks and the reproaching laughter. In her presence she felt like a little girl, ashamed and embarrassed, too afraid to speak up.

Georgiana sighed and got up. At least there was one place she needn't be ashamed of herself. She reached for the bell-pull to summon a maid to help her change.

She was going to the music room.

*****

Thaddeus Crosby entered the house after a long horseback ride around the countryside. He handed his hat and gloves to a footman and inquired after the whereabouts of the residents. Upon learning that the guests that had arrived that afternoon were resting and the family was in the sitting room, he made his way to his chambers to change from his riding clothes.

Once he had done so, he resigned himself to joining his brother and sister-in-law in the sitting room. He had avoided them for most of the day, preferring his mount's uncritical company. He shook his head as he made his way toward the sitting room. He had no idea what had made his brother marry that woman. No amount of money was worth a life shackled to someone so obnoxious.

As he made his way down the hall, the sound of music broke into his thoughts. It drifted to him faintly; he was barely able to make out the strains. He paused and listened, trying to make it out. He knew neither his sister-in-law nor Mrs. Bingley had an affinity for the pianoforte. Intrigued, he followed the sounds, listening as the impassioned playing grew louder and louder, until finally he stood outside the music room door.

It stood slightly ajar, allowing him to peek in at the occupants. Or rather, occupant, for there was only one. She sat in profile to him, her eyes closed as she played, the movement of the music sweeping through her entire body. Her fingers flew over the keys, gliding effortlessly through the difficult notes. Her flaxen hair was swept up, but the vigor of her performance had loosened a few strands that fell to frame her face and curl at the nape of her neck.

He caught his breath at the ethereal beauty before him. He had never seen anyone play with such passion and he found himself caught up in the emotion displayed. It seemed only moments later that she brought the piece to its finale, and opened her eyes as she lingered over the last notes.

Unconsciously, he took a step forward, and the movement drew her attention. Startled, her eyes widened and she stood up, shoving the bench away from the pianoforte.

Caught in the act, he entered the room, and bowed over her hand. "Excuse me. I did not mean to interrupt you." He gave her a chagrined smile. "I couldn't help but admire your playing."

Georgiana stared at the man in front of her, still a little too flustered at his abrupt appearance to immediately answer. He was of medium height, not as tall as her brother, but still taller than most men of her acquaintance. His curly, chestnut hair stood wildly in all directions, as if he had just raked his hand through it. To be sure, as she watched, he ran his hand through his hair again. His eyes, upon first inspection, appeared a most ordinary brown. But as he glanced at her questioningly, she realized the brown gradually transformed to the most brilliant teal as it approached his pupil. She gave herself a small shake and endeavored to give him a friendly smile.

"I'm sorry if I disturbed you with my playing," she answered. "I was led to believe that only the family was in residence."

He grinned back at her. "Well, I suppose in a way I am one of the family. I don't believe we've been introduced, and as there is no one else around to do the job for us, I suppose we'll have to make our own introductions." He bowed at the waist. "I am Mr. Thaddeus Crosby, younger brother of Mr. Alfred Crosby."

Georgiana couldn't help but smile back at his good humor. "Miss Georgiana Darcy, sir. It is a pleasure to make your acquaintance," she replied with a curtsy.

Thaddeus joined her at the pianoforte, where she seated herself at the bench once more. Leaning on the top of the instrument he said with a rakish grin, "Ah, so you're one of the illustrious Darcys of Pemberley I've heard so much about."

She laughed and started picking out an easy tune on the keys. "We're really not as impressive as we're made out to be."

"I have no doubt that you are all ordinary people, with only the occasional talent among you," he teased. There was a lull in the conversation as he listened to her playing. "I don't suppose you play duets, do you?" he asked.

Surprised, her hands stilled on the keys and she looked up at him. Slowly, she replied, "Very rarely, and normally only with my sister, Mrs. Darcy." A twinkle appeared in her eyes. "Occasionally, I have played with my brother as well."

He came around the instrument. "If you have no objections, I'd like to join you."

She hesitated at the impropriety of such a suggestion, searching his eyes for some hint of his motive. Suddenly, a loud and obnoxious voice broke in from the doorway.

"There you are Mr. Crosby!" Caroline called. "And Miss Darcy, as well," she acknowledged grudgingly. She floated into the room to give Georgiana an artificial embrace. "It is so good to see you again, of course."

Georgiana responded politely and Caroline turned to look at her brother-in-law, "Brother dear, do come join us in the sitting room. We are about to sit down to tea."

Thaddeus agreed reluctantly, and Caroline latched on to his arm possessively. "Won't you join us Miss Darcy?" he asked, offering her his other arm.

She made a show of gathering some sheet music. "I'll be along in just a few moments. I have a few things to put away in here first. You go on without me."

Thaddeus cast one last glance back at her as they exited the room. Finally, they were gone, and Georgiana abandoned her pretense and collapsed back on the bench. Blushing furiously, she raised her hands to her cheeks to cool them.

How could she have acted so familiarly with a man she barely knew? He must have been shocked at her impropriety! Unbidden, a smile slid to her face at the thought of their interaction. And yet, she had found his company quite enjoyable and pleasant. There had been none of the awkwardness of her usual first encounters. Secretly, she wondered if he would renew his interest in playing a duet with her, and if she would accept if he asked again. She had a sneaking suspicion if he asked, she wouldn't turn him down.

Georgiana got up to finish putting away her music. She didn't want to tarry any longer. Even Caroline Crosby's presence couldn't keep her away from the sitting room today.

Chapter 3

Thaddeus Crosby was watching the door to the sitting room. Caroline was going on and on about something to the room in general, but he wasn't paying any attention. Surely that horrid woman couldn't have anything of importance to say. All he could think about was *her*, and when she would join them.

He had found her company quite liberating, as if they had been friends for years, not the acquaintance of a moment. He cast his mind back, trying to remember if Caroline had ever mentioned her.

He frowned, trying to sift through all the inane gossip she dispensed to pick out the tidbits he desired now. *Ah, yes.* There was of course, the general Darcy information, rich as Croesus and well-respected, among the first circles, *blah, blah, blah*. But she had also mentioned Miss Darcy being quite accomplished, and especially talented on the pianoforte.

That was an understatement if there ever was one, he thought. There was something more though, niggling at the back of his mind.

The sound of the door opening cut off his train of thought and he straightened in his chair, peering eagerly at the door. A petite, dark-haired lady with dancing brown eyes and a tall, elegant gentleman appeared around the corner. He slumped back in his seat, disappointed.

The couple was introduced to him as Mr. and Mrs. Darcy. As they expressed their delight in meeting him, he sat back up in his chair and made an effort to be polite and friendly, keeping one eye on the door. It wouldn't do to make a bad impression on the renowned Darcys.

Finally, Thaddeus noticed the door opening unobtrusively, and Georgiana slid quietly into the room. He watched her covertly as she made her way over to join the group her brother and sister were conversing with.

Elizabeth turned to welcome her as Georgiana slipped into a chair next to her.

"Georgiana, dear, allow me introduce you to our new acquaintance, Mr. Thaddeus Crosby. He is Mr. Crosby's brother. Mr. Crosby, this is my sister, Miss Georgiana Darcy," Elizabeth performed the introductions.

Thaddeus smiled. "I feel obliged to inform you, Mrs. Darcy, that we have already met. I stumbled upon Miss Darcy in the music room not half an hour ago."

Elizabeth and Darcy turned toward Georgiana, surprised. Elizabeth raised her eyebrows and looked at her expectantly.

Georgiana blushed prettily and replied, "I was not overly tired from the journey, so I decided to take the opportunity to practice. I hope my efforts were not too distracting, Mr. Crosby."

"I found your playing to be distracting in the best sense of the word," he replied. "I wish every young, gently bred woman put as much effort into the instrument as you do. If they did, I think I would find the drawing room to be a far less tedious place."

His comment earned him a chuckle, and Mr. Darcy replied with an unreadable glance at his wife, "Yes, I find that the word accomplished is used too freely in regard to many. To be sure, I know only a handful of such ladies who truly deserve the word."

There was a pregnant pause as Mr. and Mrs. Darcy shared a smile at the private joke while Mr. Crosby and Georgiana looked on.

Thaddeus cleared his throat, drawing their attention back to the conversation.

"Yes, well…"

He was interrupted by Caroline calling imperiously across the room, "Miss Darcy, do come join me. I simply must know how your cousin, Mrs. Fitzwilliam, is getting along."

Georgiana rose and went to join her with an apologetic look. Soon after, Elizabeth was drawn into a private conversation with her sister and Mr. Bingley. Mr. Alfred Crosby joined his brother and Mr. Darcy, and the gentlemen, being universally intelligent and well-read, were soon deep in discussion.

*****

Georgiana Darcy felt trapped. Caroline had taken her hand in an effort to appear intimate, and she was holding it in a vise-like grip, her fingernails digging into Georgiana's palm.

"Georgiana, dear," Caroline purred, "I do so hope that you haven't been subjected to many visits from the Bennets. The last time I visited Charles the Bennets were also in residence and I must say I didn't have a moment's peace the entire fortnight. I was afraid I would have an attack of nerves myself!" Her eyes took on a calculating gleam as she continued, "I must say I have never been as thankful as I was then for my dear Mr. Crosby. I don't know how I would have made it through without him. I can only imagine *your* own suffering without a husband to support you. How you must long for someone to shield you from that distastefulness!"

Caroline knew her barb had hit its mark by Georgiana's sharp intake of breath. *A two-for-one,* Georgiana thought. *She managed to insult Elizabeth's family and my unmarried state in one fell swoop.*

Georgiana's mouth thinned as she carefully worded her reply. "I find Elizabeth's family quite invigorating when they visit." She would not allow Caroline to disparage her dear sister's family, even if she didn't have the confidence to defend herself! "It is so pleasant to spend time with those who don't think too highly of themselves." She smiled sweetly at Caroline and rose triumphantly. "If you will excuse me, I just remembered some news I must share with Jane."

She swept away regally, leaving a dumbfounded Caroline in her wake.

Darcy watched from the corner of his eye as his sister, head held high, crossed the room and joined his wife and her sister, leaving an open-mouthed Caroline Crosby staring after her. As he watched, Caroline snapped her mouth shut and a look of annoyance spread across her face. He couldn't help but smile to himself. He wasn't sure where Georgiana had found the gumption to challenge Caroline, but he was not displeased with the results.

Seated beside him, Alfred Crosby suddenly frowned, realizing where Darcy's attention was focused. His quick glance at his wife revealed she was making to rise from her seat, a very unpleasant look on her face.

He grimaced and made his apologies to the group he had been conversing with, "Excuse me, gentlemen. It appears I must attend to my wife."

He quickly debunked and joined her on the settee, pulling her back down as he sat.

Darcy returned his attention to his companion only to see the young man grinning widely.

Before he could say anything, Thaddeus admitted, "It is perhaps crass of me to admit it, but seeing how you have long been acquainted with the family, I am assured you will understand. It is a rare pleasure to see someone put my sister in her place. I fear sometimes my brother is not as firm with her as he should be."

Darcy sipped his tea in order to collect his thoughts before replying, "She is not the easiest person to get along with. I sometimes find myself wondering what drew Mr. Crosby to her. It was certainly not her appealing personality!"

Thaddeus grew silent and serious before responding, "I do not claim to know my brothers thoughts, but perhaps he sees something in her that we do not."

Darcy inclined his head in acquiescence, and the two men drank their tea before moving on to more pleasant topics.

Across the room, Georgiana was greeted with a warm smile and welcomed into the discussion among Jane, Elizabeth, and Charles. She sat quietly for a few minutes, willing her heart to stop pounding and her hands to stop shaking. She felt slightly guilty for insulting Caroline, but she knew the comment was well deserved.

She was drawn back to the present by Elizabeth saying, "We were discussing the possibility of a picnic tomorrow, should the weather hold out. What do you think, Georgiana?"

Georgiana smiled. "I think that sounds lovely! Would the children be able to join us? I would hate for them to miss out on all the fun."

Jane responded, "I think that is a wonderful idea. I'm sure we can accommodate them. What do you think, Charles?"

Charles nodded. "What a capital idea! I'm sure Geoffrey would love to be included in the adult's entertainment." He smiled wryly. "Perhaps it would help keep him out of trouble for one day."

The small group laughed, while Jane blushed.

"I know Thea would love a picnic," Elizabeth chimed in, "Although Will would probably sleep through it. Darcy has been promising her one since the season ended."

The group continued their conversation, making plans for the next day, until the dressing bell rang and they all adjourned to change for dinner.

*****

Alone in her apartment, Georgiana surveyed her evening dresses with a critical eye. She wanted to look her best tonight, and she wasn't going to examine the reasons why too closely. *I always like to look my best,* she reassured herself. *Besides, I don't want to give Caroline any opportunity to taunt me tonight.*

She held a gown of sapphire blue against her body and peeked at her reflection in the looking glass. Her mercurial eyes instantly deepened to match the intense hue of the dress.

Her lady's maid entered the room and squealed in delight at the picture her mistress portrayed in the mirror.

"That dress is perfect for you, Miss! The blue brings out your eyes and contrasts perfectly with your blonde hair."

She came up behind Georgiana and narrowed her eyes, examining her reflection, and then grinned widely in delight. "I know just the style for your hair." A sly gleam came into her eye. "You'll be pretty enough to catch the eye of a prince."

Georgiana blushed, but chose to ignore the maid's comment. It wouldn't do to fuel the gossip among the servants. Instead, she instructed the woman to help her undress, and together they set about getting her ready for dinner.

*****

Thaddeus paced the confines of his room. He had dressed in record time but he couldn't be early to dinner. His valet had abandoned him when he had begun to pace, swiftly excusing himself and edging toward the door while keeping a wary eye on his master.

Thaddeus had let him go, knowing he didn't need an audience to his frustration. He threw himself down in his chair and ran his hand through his hair. He caught a glance of himself in the mirror and had to grin. He shook his head and leaned back. He couldn't believe he was so anxious for the company of a woman. He was acting like a school boy with his first crush. And he had only met Georgiana earlier that afternoon!

Yet, she was different than any other woman he had met before and he was drawn to her. There was a quiet grace and elegance about her that lent a subtlety to her words and actions. She did not command the attention of the room; indeed, she appeared to have no desire for it. But she did command his attention and respect, even if she had never asked for it. Her passion while she was playing the pianoforte had captivated him.

The idea that such a quiet, unassuming person hid such a passion within her fascinated him. Having uncovered one of her secrets, he couldn't help wondering what else there was to discover about her. He found himself quite looking forward to dinner, even if he knew that he wouldn't really be able to get to know her with everyone around. He grimaced. Especially since Caroline would be sure to try and monopolize the conversation.

He glanced up and noted the time had passed quickly while he was musing. He stood and made his way to the door. It was time to go to dinner.

*****

Georgiana scrutinized herself one last time in the mirror. She was satisfied with her appearance. She would bring no ridicule on the Darcy name that night. *And perhaps,* she thought with a twinkle, *I might even bring a little bit of admiration to the Darcy name instead.*

Giving herself one last backward glance, she turned around and left the room. It wouldn't do to be late for dinner on her first night at Chetborn.

*****

Dinner that evening was a very interesting affair. The Darcys and the Bingleys were seated next to one another and spent the duration of the meal in constant amiable conversation. The other end of the table was treated to the incessant chatter of Caroline Crosby. Thankfully, and uncharacteristically, Caroline kept her monologue on neutral grounds. This was in part due to a stern reprimand from her husband for her earlier behavior, and in part due to Caroline's complete inability to realize that none of her companions had any interest in anything she said.

Thaddeus managed to make one attempt to change the subject and draw Georgiana out, but any reply she could have made was drowned out by Caroline. He shot a glare at his brother, but Alfred Crosby just shook his head at his brother and resumed eating his meal. He knew when to pick his battles.

So Thaddeus had to be content with sneaking surreptitious glances at Georgiana and admiring her choice of gown from across the table.

For her part, Georgiana was secretly glad that Caroline was monopolizing the conversation. She was sure she wouldn't have been able to say anything remotely coherent, with Mr. Crosby staring at her like that. She blushed hotly at the subtle admiration in his eyes. She suddenly wished she hadn't worn the sapphire gown. She didn't know what to do with herself under his intense gaze. Trying desperately to ignore him, she bent her head and applied herself to her dinner. Instead of helping her regain her composure, she became a bumbling fool. She clanked her silverware against her dish, almost dropped her wine glass, and nearly spilled her soup.

She caught her brother watching her suspiciously when she dropped her spoon into her soup bowl for the third time. Embarrassed, she endeavored to bring herself under control and slid on the Darcy mask she and her brother were known for. Thankfully, no one else seemed to notice her sudden clumsiness and, with her mask firmly in place, she made it through the rest of dinner without any further incidence.

After what seemed an eternity, the ladies left the gentlemen to their port and withdrew to the drawing room.

Georgiana took a seat next to her sister with relief and complimented Jane on the lovely dinner. She smiled graciously and thanked her.

"Yes, the food was quite good, considering you don't keep a French cook like Mr. Crosby and I do," cut in Caroline.

Jane seemed to take the words at face value, and thanked Caroline gracefully. Elizabeth and Georgiana shared a look before Elizabeth sought to change the subject.

"Why don't we have the children sent for?" she suggested. "I'm not used to being separated from my little dears for so long."

Jane agreed enthusiastically, "Yes, let's do. With the excitement of your arrival today I've hardly been able to spend any time with Geoffrey."

Even Caroline sniffed and said, "I suppose it would be pleasant to see my nephew."

Georgiana agreed wholeheartedly, and Jane got up to ring for the children to be brought down. They didn't have long to wait before the nurse came in, carrying Will Darcy, with Thea and Geoffrey in tow.

Elizabeth got up from her seat and greeted Thea with a hug, then took her baby from the nurse. Thea climbed on to Georgiana's lap and settled herself against her aunt, sucking her thumb. Being in general a quiet, subdued child, she was a little overwhelmed to be in a different house and surrounded by people she didn't know. Finding she sympathized with the shy little girl, Georgiana cuddled her close, stroking her hair soothingly.

Geoffrey Bingley had no such reservations as he rocketed across the room and flung himself unceremoniously into his mother's arms.

Jane Bingley let out an unladylike, "Oof," and sat back hard in her chair.

"Now, Geoffrey," she admonished. "What did Mama tell you about being gentle?"

He let go of his mother reluctantly. "That I hafta be very careful with Mama right now cuz I could hurt the baby inside her tummy." He rubbed her stomach gingerly. "Sorry, Baby. I be more careful."

Jane blushed bright red and shushed her son. "Yes, dear, but we don't talk about that among company." She looked up at Elizabeth with a chagrined smile and apologized, "That's not exactly how I wanted to tell you."

Elizabeth, careful not to disturb the baby on her lap, reached over to squeeze her sister's hand, beaming. "I'm so happy for you! But I can't say I didn't have my suspicions already."

Georgiana voiced her own congratulations and even Caroline seemed sincere in her delight for Jane. The women quickly began to discuss the future addition to the Bingley family and the time passed swiftly until the gentlemen joined them.

Darcy was delighted to see his daughter and son when he walked into the drawing room. He stopped briefly to share a smile with Thea and tousle her hair before sweeping his son away from Elizabeth and settling in a nearby chair. His wife shook her head at him but he just grinned cheekily and bounced Will on his knee.

The men settled down and Georgiana found herself seated next to Mr. Thaddeus Crosby. He smiled at Thea on her lap.

"Who is this lovely young lady?" he asked.

Georgiana graced him with a full, genuine smile that left him a little stunned and speechless.

"This, Mr. Crosby, is my niece, Thea Darcy," she said with obvious pride. Just the hint of a dimple in her cheek flashed briefly, before it disappeared.

Thaddeus blinked and refocused on the little girl in front of him. Thea was smiling at him around her thumb in the most discerning manner. He could have sworn the little girl knew exactly what he was thinking.

"Good evening, Miss Darcy. It is a pleasure to make your acquaintance," he said, inclining his head in her direction.

Thea popped her thumb out her mouth and batted her eyelashes at him with uncharacteristic boldness. "Pleased to meet you."

Georgiana giggled. "I do believe you have an admirer, Mr. Crosby."

Thaddeus eyed the little girl with mock wariness. "I do hope I won't have to be fending off your mother now."

Georgiana laughed. "I believe you are safe on that front Mr. Crosby. My sister is not yet intent on finding a husband for her daughter."

Thea spoke up from her lap, saying very seriously, "I'm not goin' ta get married when I grow up.

Geoff and I are goin' ta build a pirate ship and have all sorts of a'ventures."

Caught off guard, Georgiana could only blink in surprise at her niece.

Recovering a little more quickly, Thaddeus answered her equally as seriously, "That is a very noble ambition Miss Darcy. Have you considered that perhaps a husband would aid you in your endeavor to see the world? It would be very convenient to have someone around to protect your virtue when you're out fighting pirates."

Thea seemed to consider this suggestion, before she shrugged. "Maybe." Tiring of the conversation, the little girl climbed off Georgiana's lap and went to join her mother.

Georgiana smiled wryly at Thaddeus. "She's not generally quite so talkative with strangers. I had no idea her ambitions were quite so... err...*noble,* as you said sir. I do believe you've made a friend."

Thaddeus smiled back at her, but his words were serious, "A bit of spunk is not a bad thing. I daresay it will stand her in good stead with this world we live in."

Georgiana could only agree, but commented, "Perhaps a little less time spent in her cousin's company would make her dreams a little more realistic."

Thaddeus laughed. "Yes, I have noticed that young Geoffrey seems to have quite the imagination; and quite the gift for practical jokes, I must say." He seemed to be privately amused about something.

Georgiana could not contain her curiosity. "You must tell me sir, what you find so humorous."

Thaddeus looked around to see if anyone was paying any attention to them before lowering his voice to respond, "The first day we were here I came upon young Master Bingley in the hallway to the guest bedrooms, looking very guilty indeed. I questioned him as to the whereabouts of his nurse, and was just about to take him back to her, when I noticed two large, bulbous eyes peering at me from his coat pocket. Intrigued, I asked him what he was about. He proceeded to show me the frog he had caught and explained that he meant to surprise his nurse with it. I, being the gentleman I am, dissuaded him from his course. Not thinking any more of the incident, I returned the young man to his nurse and the frog to its home. However, unbeknownst to me, young Geoffrey had already made one stop before I caught up with him. That night, after dinner, my sister retired early, claiming a headache. Not long after, we were all roused from the drawing room by her screams. Apparently, Master Geoffrey had left another of his friends in her bed."

Georgiana laughed, rewarding Thaddeus with a glimpse of her dimples and briefly drawing her sister's attention. She smiled to reassure Elizabeth, before begging Thaddeus to continue.

"It was quite a sight to behold, I must say. Caroline had climbed on top of the dressing table in her room, clothed only in her nightclothes, and was screaming at the top of her lungs. Meanwhile, the frog peered placidly out from under the bedcovers, without so much as a croak. It took my brother quite awhile to calm her, but eventually I was called upon to return the creature to his natural habitat." Thaddeus' eyes twinkled. "I do believe Geoffrey has been banned from the guest wing for the time being. I can only imagine the trials his poor nurse has been enduring during our stay."

As he concluded his story, Geoffrey Bingley himself came over and stood next to Thaddeus.

"Master Geoffrey, we were just discussing you and your friends the frogs. Tell me, what have you been doing since last I saw you?" Thaddeus asked.

"Not'ing much," the little boy pouted. "I'm not allowed anywheres 'cepting for the nursery without Mama and Papa being there."

He brightened a little. "But today Thea came and I got to tell her all about the mean lady." Here he sent a glare in Caroline's direction. "And how she screamed and screamed and screamed when I put Mr. Jumper in her bed. And we talked about pirates and treasure and lots of other stuff."

He peered up at Mr. Crosby. "Did you know she's got a pony?" Without waiting for an answer he grumbled, "I want a pony. How comes I don't got a pony and she does?"

"Perhaps you could ask your parents if you could have a pony," Thaddeus pointed out helpfully.

The little boy grinned eagerly at him. "Say, that's not a bad idea, Mr. Crosby!" He skipped off excitedly to accost his parents.

"I don't think his parents will thank you for giving him that idea, Mr. Crosby," Georgiana admonished with a smile. "Don't you think he's a little young for a pony?"

"Perhaps a little," Thaddeus admitted. "He does have a tendency to get himself in trouble as it is. But your niece is the same age and she has a pony, so I hardly see what your complaint is."

"That is true," Georgiana allowed. "But my brother has had her on horseback since before she could walk. He is insistent that she will not develop the fear of horses that her mother has. Geoffrey has hardly had the same introduction that she has."

"I can see the advantage of introducing her to horses at such a young age. Tell me, Miss Darcy, do you share the same love of horseback riding?" Thaddeus asked.

"I do enjoy it," she responded, "but I admit that I have developed the same love for walking that my sister has. There is nothing better for clearing my mind when something troubles me."

"After witnessing you at the pianoforte this afternoon I would have thought that music would be your preferred outlet for clearing your mind," Thaddeus commented.

"I do turn to music, but I find it is better for releasing frustration than clearing my mind. There is something about the serenity of nature that just soothes the mind and body," Georgiana said.

"I have to agree with you," Thaddeus admitted, "Although I have to say I prefer a horseback ride to a walk when I need to clear my head."

"Ah, but you have an advantage when it comes to riding. It is hardly proper for a gentlewoman to be seen galloping willy-nilly over the countryside, while no one thinks twice of a gentleman doing the same. You cannot expect me to derive the same benefits you would," Georgiana corrected him.

"I would think that Pemberley would not be so short of acreage that you need fear being seen out riding, Miss Darcy, and criticized," Thaddeus commented.

"So you would think," Georgiana sighed, reflecting on past experiences.

"I can see then, how you would find walking to be preferable. Do you often find it necessary to engage in that activity?" Thaddeus asked.

Georgiana smiled. "It depends on the circumstances."

Thaddeus laughed. "Do you think the circumstances will be favorable for a few walks during your visit?"

Her eyes twinkled at him, but as she opened her mouth to answer him her niece interrupted them with a pout. "Mama says I have to say goodnight, Aunt Giana."

"Then come give me a hug, dear." Georgiana opened her arms, and Thea gave her a quick squeeze. "What do you say to Mr. Crosby now?"

"G'night, Mr. Crosby," Thea said seriously, with her best curtsey, which was still quite wobbly.

"Good night, Miss Darcy," he answered, equally seriously. "I do hope you have pleasant dreams."

The little girl nodded and went off with the servant that had been sent to collect her and the other children. Soon after, the Darcys and the Bingleys excused themselves to tuck their children into bed and make their way to their chambers themselves.

Georgiana was beginning to feel the effects of her long day. She tried to stifle a yawn, but Mr. Crosby was watching her knowingly. She smiled ruefully and stood. "I fear that the long day has finally caught up with me. Please excuse me, Mr. Crosby." She curtsied and made her excuses to the rest of the room before sweeping out gracefully.

Thaddeus found himself in an inexplicably good mood as he retired for the night soon after. Suddenly, he was rather looking forward to the remainder of his time at Chetborn.

Chapter 4

Georgiana woke, refreshed, to see the light of early morning obscured by a gray drizzle. She sighed. There would be no picnic that day after all. She climbed out of the bed, wrapped herself in her dressing gown, and made her way to the window. She watched briefly as the rain ran in rivulets down the pane, tracing patterns on the glass, and then focused on the landscape beyond. There were a few servants scurrying from the stables to the kitchens in the main house, but for the most part the grounds were empty, water pooling on the walkways.

Georgiana turned back into the room to get dressed. A little while later, very simply clad in a gray morning dress to match the day, having managed to get ready on her own, she made her way to the library. She noted the quiet of the great house with pleasure as she made her way through the hallways.

She appreciated the solitude that the early morning afforded her. At home in Pemberley, her brother and sister would already have risen and would be either enjoying a walk together or companionably caring for their correspondence in the morning room. Although she knew that the privacy would not last, Elizabeth and Darcy both normally being early risers, she would take the opportunity the hard day of traveling the day before provided her.

She entered the library to find the great room quite deserted, but she had not expected it to be otherwise. Slowly, she made her way along the bookshelves. The room was not as well-stocked as Pemberley's library, but it was evident that Jane Bingley had put some effort into improving the selection; she doubted Mr. Bingley would have thought of it himself. She meandered along until she found a book she was interested in, taking it with her over to the window seat on the far side of the room.

Knowing she was unlikely to be disturbed, she kicked off her slippers and curled up on the seat. She took one last look out the large window at the dreary day, and then turned her thoughts to more pleasant things as she opened her book.

An hour or so later, Georgiana set the book aside and turned to peer out the window. With a sigh, she noted that the rain was coming down harder and the wind had picked up. The chiming of the clock drew her attention as her stomach grumbled. With a smile, she realized that breakfast would be being served now. Setting aside her book, she slid back on her slippers and eagerly made her way to the breakfast room.

She entered the breakfast room and was slightly taken aback to find it still empty. She made herself a plate before sitting down to a leisurely breakfast with the morning paper all to herself.

*****

Thaddeus Crosby was not a morning person. He made his way down the hallways to the breakfast room half awake, his hair mussed despite the best attempts of his valet. He was a surprised upon entering to find Georgiana the only occupant of the room. Engrossed in the paper, she did little more than glance in his direction before refocusing on the page in front of her.

Still somewhat groggy, he filled his plate from the sideboard and poured himself a cup of steaming coffee before sitting down beside Georgiana. He cupped his hands around his mug and took a whiff of the invigorating brew. Just the scent seemed to perk him up some and he took a sip before digging into his meal.

They continued this way for a time until Thaddeus, feeling quite a bit livelier after his second cup of coffee, addressed Georgiana, "Miss Darcy, I don't suppose you would share some of the paper?"

Georgiana looked up somewhat guiltily from where she had been monopolizing the paper.

"Of course, Mr. Crosby," she acquiesced reluctantly, handing over the sections she had read.

"You must excuse me for not offering to share earlier. I was quite absorbed in what I was reading."

"I noticed," he commented. "You hardly even looked up when I entered the room."

Taking the pages she offered, they returned to their companionable silence, each immersed in the paper before them.

Elizabeth and Darcy found them still in the same manner sometime later. Elizabeth seated herself across from her sister while Darcy filled their plates.

"Good morning, Georgiana. I trust you slept well?" Elizabeth greeted her sister.

"Very well," Georgiana murmured, still distracted by the paper.

"And you as well, Mr. Crosby?" Elizabeth asked, as Darcy set her plate in front of her and took his place beside her.

Thaddeus looked up and smiled at the couple in front of him. "I did sleep well, Mrs. Darcy. I hope you and Mr. Darcy were able to as well."

Darcy accepted a section of the paper from Thaddeus and fell to considering it silently while he ate, eerily like his sister. His wife, however, was determined to have some conversation at the table.

"I fear our picnic is out of the question for today, as well as any outdoor activities, with the rain," Elizabeth commented.

Georgiana murmured, "Mmm Hmm," and Darcy grunted, but it was Thaddeus who answered, the amusement evident in his voice, "Yes, I think we are to be confined indoors today. Hopefully, we will be able to entertain ourselves."

They were soon joined by Charles and Jane Bingley and Alfred Crosby. Caroline had opted to have breakfast sent to her room on a tray. With the additions to the party, the conversation flowed smoothly and Georgiana and Darcy were left to peruse the paper in peace.

Finally, everyone finished eating breakfast and the party broke up, each of them to pursue their own activities. Georgiana made her way to the music room, thinking to use the time inside to practice. She sat down at the pianoforte and began to warm up, playing some scales and then some simple melodies.

She was just beginning an intricate piece by Mozart when Thaddeus appeared in the doorway, a book in hand.

"I hope you don't mind my joining you," he said as he crossed the room to take a seat near the windows. "I find the music soothing. I promise you will hardly know I'm here."

Georgiana merely nodded as she continued playing. More self-conscious with an audience, she did not play with her usual abandon, but the performance was no less enjoyable for her spectator.

About half an hour later, they heard a ruckus from the hallway, and Caroline's shrill voice, demanding to know where Mr. Crosby was. Unsure which Mr.

Crosby she was referring to, Thaddeus scooted his chair a little further toward the window, where he would not be seen from the hallway. He watched the doors anxiously as Georgiana played on, seemingly oblivious to the commotion outside.

When Caroline passed by with barely a glimpse at the room, he sighed audibly and relaxed in his chair.

Georgiana gave him an amused glance, but waited until she was sure Caroline would not return before she brought the piece to a close.

"I think, Mr. Crosby, that it was not the soothing music that drew you to this room," she teased gently.

"No?" he questioned, innocently, before admitting, "But it certainly is one of the advantages."

He grinned slyly at her. "It is very quiet and peaceful in here compared to some of the more occupied rooms of the house."

In the distance, they heard Caroline's sharp voice carrying down the hallway. Georgiana quickly began to play again, covering her voice as she said, "You need not fear, Mr. Crosby. Your hiding place is safe with me."

Thaddeus smiled back at her gratefully and returned to his book. They continued on in their separate pursuits until Georgiana brought her practice to a close just as Thaddeus turned the last page in his book.

"I fear I can provide you refuge no longer, Mr. Crosby," Georgiana said as she began to put away her music.

Thaddeus closed his book and replied, "That is quite alright, Miss Darcy. I appreciated the reprieve while it lasted. I think I shall head to the library to find another book. May I escort you to your next destination along the way?"

"As my destination is the same as yours, you may. I left the book I was reading in the library earlier this morning," Georgiana commented, accepting the arm he offered to her.

They traversed the great house, speaking quietly so as not to draw attention to themselves. Upon entering the room, they were pleasantly surprised to find it occupied by Mr. and Mrs. Darcy, seated by the fireplace.

Darcy noted his sister's entrance on Thaddeus' arm with a slight furrowing of his brow. Elizabeth merely raised an eyebrow in response and shook her head warningly at her husband.

"Have you finished practicing, Georgiana?" Elizabeth greeted her sister.

"I have. I remembered I had left my book on the window seat earlier, and since Mr. Crosby was headed this way also, he was so good as to accompany me," Georgiana explained, knowing what her brother and sister were thinking.

"That was kind of you Mr. Crosby," Elizabeth acknowledged, seeming to accept the explanation at face value. The glance she shared with her husband as Thaddeus went to peruse the bookshelves and

Georgiana returned to the window seat, however, belied that assumption.

Aware of the company, Georgiana did not return to her earlier position on the window seat, but demurely perched on the edge as she sought her book from where she had stored it earlier. She settled into the seat with her book and soon lost herself in its pages.

Thaddeus watched Georgiana surreptitiously as he ostensibly scanned the shelves for a book. She seemed to be completely immersed in what she was reading, oblivious to everyone around her. Mr. and Mrs. Darcy, on the other hand, were communicating silently over the top of their books.

Amused, Thaddeus picked a tome of the shelf at random and went to sit near the Darcy's, effectively cutting off their communication. He opened his book and turned to the first page, noticing from the corner of his eye as the Darcys sat back in their chairs, shooting him twin disgruntled looks.

He struggled to hide his smile behind the volume in his hand. Thankfully, the Darcy's were too involved in their own annoyance to notice the fun he was having at their expense. He settled in to enjoy his book, surprised to find it discussed various farming methods. He mentally shrugged. It was better than it could have been, considering he had selected it by chance. At this stage in his life, it probably wouldn't hurt him to learn more about agriculture anyway.

He fell to considering the information, but it wasn't long after that Mrs. Darcy drew him into conversation.

"I see you've chosen a volume on agriculture, Mr. Crosby. Do you have an estate you're seeking to improve?" Elizabeth inquired, her intent in asking the question obvious.

"Not yet, Mrs. Darcy," Thaddeus replied easily. "Although I plan to change that shortly. In the meantime, I can only seek to improve myself in order to become a more competent landlord."

"Then you have chosen wisely," Mr. Darcy commented. "I have implemented many of the methods suggested in that book, with fine outcomes. I particularly recommend the ideas found in chapter 15. The changes I made based on them resulted in some very high yields this past harvest."

Impressed, Thaddeus thanked Darcy for his insight and looked at the volume in his hand with a new appreciation. The older man just nodded in recognition. He had had to learn to manage an estate on his own, mostly through trial and error. If he could help lighten the load even a little, then he was happy to do so.

Soon thereafter, Thaddeus questioned Darcy about a technique for crop rotation mentioned in the book, and the two men quickly became absorbed in a discussion on farming methods.

Elizabeth eventually grew bored with their conversation and moved to a chair nearer her sister. She knew better than to try to interrupt Georgiana when she was immersed in a book, but the younger woman had not been as absorbed as she had seemed since she looked up with a smile and said, "Have you and my brother spent all morning in the library?"

"The majority of it, yes," Elizabeth replied. "I had some correspondence to take care of and Will had some business letters he wanted to look through privately. We thought to join the others in the drawing room soon, but I think your brother has settled in for the time being." She smiled ruefully. "I can't blame him for seeking a little solitude when he can find it. You know he is not always his best in company."

Georgiana nodded, knowing exactly how her brother felt. She rose and said, "Nonetheless, I should join the others. I fear I've been neglecting our hosts. My presence should buy you and Will a little more time before you are expected to appear."

Elizabeth reached up to touch her arm as she made to leave. "Thank you dear. I know your brother will appreciate it."

Georgiana responded with a smile before she exited the room, book in hand.

Thaddeus vaguely noticed her exit, deep in conversation with Darcy. He was a little disappointed to see her go, but he understood the obligation to join the others in their party. Elizabeth remained, which he found somewhat unusual, given that most of the women he knew would have left behind their husbands long ago for the gossip of the drawing room. But he had noticed the deep regard between the Darcys, and he could not help but hope that someday his wife would be equally as loathe to be separated from him.

The two men continued their conversation until Darcy eventually noticed his wife staring out the window at the water dripping down the pane. Correctly interpreting her pose as boredom, he suggested that they join the others in the drawing room, resigned to the necessity. Elizabeth smiled gratefully at her husband. Being of a much more social nature than him, she was looking forward to spending some time in the more varied company, especially with her sister among them.

Thaddeus declined the Darcys' offer to join them, explaining he had some letters of business to write before he joined the others. Understanding, they left him to his correspondence.

When they had left, Thaddeus sat alone, one hand on the book in his lap, staring out into space. It was true that he had business to attend to, but he knew that he was using it as an excuse to avoid Caroline's company for a little longer. He sighed. Since they had been at Chetborn, Caroline seemed to think that he was there to see to her personal entertainment. He had spent most of his time outside in an attempt to evade her. He smiled to himself. Caroline was not an outdoors type. Even if she did venture into the gardens, he could easily outdistance her.

He got up to attend to his business affairs. However reluctant he was to be around Caroline, the Darcy's and the Bingley's company made it tolerable.

*****

Georgiana made a quick stop in her room to pick up some embroidery she was working on before continuing toward the drawing room. Soon, she was able to make out the sharp strains of Caroline's voice. The closer she got, the louder Caroline's voice became, and the more the muscles in her neck and shoulders tensed.

Georgiana paused outside the door, able to clearly make out Caroline's words. The footman made to open the door for her, but she stayed him with the lift of her hand.

"Just a moment, please," she requested softly. He acknowledged her appeal by returning to his position beside the door, hands folded, back stiff. She thought she detected a hint of sympathy in his gaze, but it was quickly schooled into a blank, subservient expression. She briefly wished wistfully for the familiar faces of Pemberley and the general amiability and openness that existed between the servants and the residents.

The servants here obviously thought her to be like many members of the ton, having little regard for those in their employ and preferring to see the results of their work without acknowledging the hard labor behind it. She sighed. It was sad, really, but she knew it was normal for many families in high society.

She schooled her features into a mask of demure equanimity and squared her shoulders, then nodded to the footman. He opened the door to admit her and she glided into the room with all the poise she possessed, head held high.

Her entrance immediately drew Caroline's attention.

"It's so kind of you to grace us with your presence this afternoon, Georgiana," she commented sarcastically.

Jane shot Georgiana a look of apology from where she sat near Caroline, but made no effort to curb the other woman's tongue. Georgiana couldn't blame her. She was probably exhausted from fending off the barbs Caroline had been throwing her way already. She felt a tinge of guiltiness for avoiding the drawing room for so long. She had left poor Jane with no one else to support her. The woman was already of a mild and gentle spirit. She hated conflict. On top of that, she was expecting, which meant she would tire more easily. Georgiana knew from experiencing Elizabeth's pregnancies that the state could cause a woman's nerves to become easily frazzled.

Georgiana chose not to respond to Caroline's acerbic comment. She smiled genially at Caroline and took a seat near Jane. The two gentlemen had ensconced themselves near the window, and appeared to be deep in conversation.

"How are you feeling today, Jane?" she asked, trying to shift the focus off of Caroline.

Jane smiled gratefully. "I was feeling a bit wan this morning but I'm feeling much better now, thank you. I heard you in the music room earlier. Were you able to practice as much as you wanted to?"

"I was able to get a lot of uninterrupted time, so I was able to work on some more difficult pieces. You have a beautiful pianoforte," Georgiana commented.

Jane blushed. "Charles just bought it. I never learned to play, but we hope that any future daughters we have will have the opportunity to be taught."

With a happier topic in mind, Georgiana asked, "Are you hoping for a girl this time?"

Jane eagerly began talking about her impending bundle of joy, and even Caroline was able to join in with equanimity, although she still managed to sneak in a few snide remarks about Jane's upbringing. The time passed fairly pleasantly until Elizabeth and Will joined them. Will immediately headed to join the men by the window while Elizabeth joined her sisters and Caroline.

Now the only one missing was Thaddeus, and Caroline immediately asked after him, "Have you seen my brother, Mr. Crosby recently? He was supposed to play a few hands of cards with me today."

Georgiana shared a glance with her sister before focusing on the needlework in her hand. She was sure that request had come more in the form of an order.

"I believe he said he had some letters of business to take care of before he joined us," Elizabeth demurred.

Caroline knew this to be true. The young man did indeed have many matters of business to care for, especially as he was looking into acquiring an estate of his own in the near future. She could only let out an exasperated huff and hope that the addition of Mr. and Mrs. Darcy to their party would bring about a more animated exchange. The conversation had been far too domestic for her childless sensibilities for too long.

Georgiana, on the other hand, recognized this tactic more for its intended purpose. She had no doubt that Mr. Crosby did have some matters of business he could attend to, but having witnessed his evasive maneuvers that morning, she was more inclined to believe this latest excuse to be more of the same. While she could understand the desire to steer clear of the drawing room, she could not help but be a little annoyed at his lack of decorum in avoiding their hosts.

Georgiana turned her attention to her embroidery and contributed little to the conversation going on around her. When Thaddeus did finally enter the room, she greeted him coolly.

Thaddeus was somewhat taken aback by the reproachful glance Georgiana threw his way. Unable to seat himself near her in order to immediately satisfy his curiosity, he joined the other men and had to be content to bid his time.

Eventually, tea was served, along with some light refreshments. Jane vacated her seat to serve the tea, and Thaddeus brought his cup over and took the empty seat. Georgiana seemed content to ignore him, silently sipping her tea.

Thaddeus leaned back in his seat and regarded her for a moment.

He took a sip of his tea, and asked nonchalantly, "Have I done something to offend you, Miss Darcy?"

Her eyes flew to meet his over the lip of her tea cup as she coughed on the sip she had just taken. She set her drink aside, not having expected to be called out for her earlier behavior. The rules of etiquette demanded he turn a blind eye to such things. Apparently, he wasn't one to abide by the rules.

"Why would you think that, Mr. Crosby?" she replied archly, one eyebrow raised.

"Miss Darcy, I have often seen my mother give my father the very same look you directed at me when I entered the room. There can only be one interpretation. I have offended you in some way. Now, I wish to make amends, but I can only do so if you explain to me what I have done wrong," Thaddeus commented.

Georgiana did not like conflict. In fact, she avoided it at all costs. She regarded the man in front of her warily, sizing him up.

Thaddeus had no such reservations. He preferred to resolve his conflicts as quickly and easily as he could. In so doing, he could be quite tenacious. Like a dog with a bone, he would not give up until he had reached a resolution. He watched the woman in front of him openly, waiting for her to make the first move.

Initially, he was afraid she was going to shut him out and pretend nothing had ever happened. Her expression was closed as she eyed him.

Georgiana wavered, her mask in place. Her inherent response was to withdraw, to hide what she was thinking. But for some reason, she felt compelled to be completely open and honest with the man in front of her, regardless of the conflict that might result.

Thaddeus could see the change in her as soon as she made the decision to open up to him. There was a hint of shyness in her eyes, but there was also a glint of determination and pride. Her chin came up, and she set her jaw stubbornly.

The flush of righteous indignation on her cheeks and the sparkle in her eye took his breath away. She was beautiful.

Not the usual, delicate porcelain beauty the ton preferred. But a real, passionate, vibrant beauty that seemed to exude from her very pores. He had seen the same passion at the pianoforte when she had thought herself unobserved. To have it focused on him was overwhelming.

He took a deep breath and worked to direct his attention to the issue at hand. He noticed the tilt of her chin and had to hide the smile that sprang to his lips. She obviously thought she was in the right, whatever it was he had done. But the smile soon died on his lips as the seriousness of her words permeated his usually jovial demeanor.

"Mr. Crosby, I'm sure you are aware that Mrs. Bingley is in a rather delicate condition." She paused to confirm this fact, and he nodded. She lowered her voice. "Yet, you chose to oblige her to entertain your sister for the entire morning."

She held up a hand to silence him as he opened his mouth to defend himself.

"I am well aware, Mr. Crosby, of the, shall we say, impositions, that Mrs. Crosby places on us all. But I don't think you fully realize the toll they take on others when you selfishly avoid her presence." Here she glanced meaningfully at Mrs. Bingley, who he hated to admit, did look a little peaked. "Not to mention that it is rather discourteous to abandon your hosts in such a way after they have graciously invited you into their home. I am not saying that you cannot spend some time with your own diversions. I am just saying you should be a little more sensitive to the needs of others."

Thaddeus was indeed ashamed to realize that he had been neglecting the Bingleys, and that more importantly, he had neglected to consider anyone's feelings besides his own. It was humbling to have this slip of a woman take him down a notch.

He admitted as much to the young woman in front of him and apologized. Georgiana was not one to hold a grudge, and having vented her frustration at him and realizing he was sincerely embarrassed, she quickly forgave him.

Thaddeus was surprised at the change in the woman in front of him. One moment she was regarding him with a decidedly chilly expression and the next she was gracing him with a sincere smile. He shook his head. He would never understand women.

Regardless, they were able to move on to more pleasant topics as they enjoyed their tea.

"What are you and Miss Darcy discussing, Mr. Crosby?" Caroline broke in on their conversation.

Thaddeus tamped down the surge of irritation that went through him at the grating sound of her voice. He met Georgiana's intense gaze. She was obviously watching to see how he would react and if he would act on their earlier conversation.

Although reluctant, he turned to Caroline with a sigh. "It was hardly anything significant, Mrs. Crosby. We were just discussing some of the merits of poetry versus novels. Do you have an opinion on the subject?"

Caroline was delighted to have the opportunity to share her opinions, and went on for some length of time. In fact, it wasn't until the bell rang to signify it was time to change for dinner that she finally quit talking. Georgiana and Thaddeus exchanged wry smiles, but Thaddeus was glad to note the glint of approval in her eye as she rose to leave the room.

"I enjoyed our conversation, Mr. Crosby. I hope we will be able to continue our discussion sometime soon," Georgiana told him, a shy smile upon her face as she paused before exiting.

Thaddeus was left remaining with a ridiculously silly smile on his face. Eventually though, he was able to rouse himself from his chair to get changed. It was fortunate for Thaddeus that everyone was far too concerned with their wardrobe choices for the evening to notice his expression, or they might have guessed his thoughts.

*****

Dinner that night was a fairly comfortable affair. The seating arrangement was the same as the night before and the conversation began much the same, at least on Georgiana's end of the table.

At any rate, tonight Georgiana was more at ease at the table. She wasn't fumbling with her utensils and threatening the cleanliness of her clothes with food and drink. She was poised, even though she could still feel Thaddeus' eyes upon her occasionally.

Thaddeus, for his part, changed his tactics from the previous night in his mission to draw Georgiana out. Instead, he took the initiative to draw his brother into the conversation. He knew Caroline would pause before interrupting her husband, if he could just get him to talk.

"Alfred, did you speak to your steward about the property in Hertfordshire you were looking at?" he asked.

Alfred glanced across the table at his wife, who compressed her lips unhappily, but was silent. "I spoke to him about it," he said shortly.

"Have you made a decision?" he asked innocently, obviously unaware of the now palpable tension between Mr. and Mrs. Crosby.

Georgiana looked nervously between the two of them and wisely held her tongue.

Alfred, shot a dark look at his brother and returned to eating. "Not yet," he replied.

Thaddeus looked confused, and made another attempt to draw his brother out. Alfred and Caroline exchanged a look over the table, and after another short answer, the table fell into silence. Even Caroline was subdued. Thaddeus glanced at Georgiana, perplexed, and met her sympathetic gaze. Maybe he could ask her later what was going on, since he was obviously missing something.

Dinner wrapped up fairly quickly after that. Again, the children were sent for and the men did not linger over their port. Georgiana was cuddling Will Darcy when the gentlemen joined them. Thaddeus found his way to Georgiana fairly quickly, with only a few minor conversations hindering his progress toward her.

She greeted him with a smile, bouncing the grinning baby on her knee. "Mr. Crosby, I see you have come over to meet the rest of my family. This is my nephew, the illustrious William Darcy of Pemberley."

"I have," he played along. He offered the baby a finger, which he eagerly grasped and immediately stuck in his mouth. Georgiana hurried to gently disengage his fingers, embarrassed when he held up the slobbery digits.

"I'm so sorry, Mr. Crosby," she apologized. "I'm afraid he's teething. Anything you hand him immediately goes into his mouth." She pulled out a handkerchief and handed it across to him. "I hope you will forgive the impropriety."

He accepted the handkerchief and used it to mop up his soiled fingers. "I think I can forgive young Mr. Darcy for his indiscretion if you will enlighten me as to what occurred over dinner this evening."

Thaddeus found himself treated to the same sympathetic gaze he had observed at dinner.

"I *think* I can shed some light on the subject for you," she replied, somewhat hesitantly. She shifted the baby on her lap to a more comfortable position as he began to doze off. "You may not be aware that Mrs. Darcy and Mrs. Bingley were originally from Hertfordshire. Longbourn, to be specific. Mr. Bingley had leased a manor in the nearby country and invited my brother to join him there. Mrs. Crosby was in attendance as well, as she was acting as mistress for her brother. It was during their time in the country that my brother and Mr. Bingley met their wives."

Georgiana paused in her story and glanced at Thaddeus sideways, not sure how much he knew about his sister-in-law prior to her marriage to his brother. Should she reveal the designs Caroline had had upon her brother? Surely, they had been public knowledge, for Caroline had made no attempt to hide her blatant efforts. Her attentions had even spread to engulf Georgiana in an attempt to win her brother's favor. Yet, would it be a terrible faux pas to tell Mr. Crosby that his brother's wife had been intent on marrying another man before she met him? How would he feel about that?

Thaddeus, for his part, was beginning to understand why the mention of Hertfordshire had caused such a disturbance at dinner.

Georgiana continued, choosing her words ever so carefully, "At the time, Mrs. Crosby, then Miss Bingley, made it very clear she desired a match between our two houses. When my brother married Elizabeth, I'm afraid she was none too pleased. Mr. Bingley's match with Jane was also frowned upon, due to her lack of fortune and connections." Here she afforded him that same sympathetic look again. "I'm afraid she does not look back on her time in Hertfordshire too fondly, which is probably the reason for the tension between your brother and sister at the dinner table this evening."

Thaddeus nodded and leaned back in his chair, silent as he contemplated what she had told him. If his brother was indeed considering purchasing an estate in Hertfordshire as an escape from London, then he could well imagine why Caroline would be upset. At the same time, the area allowed his brother to enjoy the pleasures of country life while still being an easy distance from town.

Apart from that, he also knew the property was being offered at a very tempting price, as the owner had racked up some hefty gambling debts, making him eager to sell. He could see why his brother was torn. Despite Caroline's demanding personality, he knew his brother did genuinely care for his wife (even if Thaddeus himself didn't understand it), and wanted to make her happy. But the property was too good of an opportunity to pass up.

Thaddeus sighed and made to rise. "I think I realize my error now. Thank you for explaining it to me, Miss Darcy. I think I am going to go and try to repair some of the damage I've inflicted."

Georgiana nodded as he bowed and excused himself. She snuggled her nephew closer and settled back into her seat to watch the goings on around her. She was content observing her family, even if she wasn't actively engaged in the conversation.

Will held Thea on his lap as he and Elizabeth chatted with Charles, Jane, and Caroline. Geoffrey was standing impatiently beside his father, eying Thea. Thea was actively ignoring him. Apparently, Geoffrey had done something to offend his cousin earlier in the day, Georgiana reflected with amusement.

She only glanced at Thaddeus and Mr. Crosby briefly. The two men were deep in an animated, if low-voiced, conversation. She looked away and returned to studying her family, feeling slightly embarrassed for watching what she had no doubt was a very private discussion.

The rest of the evening was spent in much the same vein as it began, with amicable conversation and a relaxed attitude. Georgiana retired that night content, happy with the time spent in good company.

*****

Late that night, Elizabeth was snuggled against Darcy's side, her head on his chest. She was nearly asleep, hovering in the haze between consciousness and slumber.

"Do you think there is any interest between Mr. Crosby and Georgiana?" Darcy asked her, worriedly. He had been lying in the darkness, working up the courage to ask her for some time.

"Hmmm…" Elizabeth murmured, rousing from sleep.

"Do you think that Mr. Crosby and Georgiana are interested in each other?" Darcy repeated.

"I doubt it, dear," she muttered, disgruntled, "seeing as he is already married."

"Not that Mr. Crosby!" he exclaimed irritably. "Mr. Thaddeus Crosby."

"I know." Elizabeth sighed, resigning herself to the fact that her husband wasn't going to let the subject drop. She patted him on the chest. "I think it is a little early to be speculating, dear. But they do seem to enjoy each other's company."

Darcy fell silent, brooding. Elizabeth gratefully drifted off again, but it was a long time before Darcy was able to find sleep.

Chapter 5

Elizabeth stretched luxuriously beside her husband in bed, trying her best not to disturb him. She knew he had not slept well the night before, since his tossing and turning had woke her several times. She felt him start to stir beside her, and turned over reluctantly to face him. He opened his eyes and smiled gently at her, drawing her closer to him.

"G'morning, dear," he murmured, stroking his hand along her hip. Elizabeth smiled. It was always a joy to wake up beside her husband. He never failed to greet her lovingly every morning. It still amazed her that after five years of marriage he still treasured those first few moments of the day with her.

It took Darcy a little longer to fully wake up than it took Elizabeth, who was already wide awake. Elizabeth took the opportunity to revel in those few precious minutes before he recalled what had been keeping him up the night before.

All too soon, a frown marred his features and his hold on her waist tightened. Elizabeth sighed. She knew Darcy was overly protective of his little sister, but he was going to have to get used to the idea of her being on her own sooner or later.

Mr. Crosby seemed a nice enough fellow. Granted, they had only known the man a few days, but Darcy had enjoyed conversing with him before he realized that the man was showing interest in his sister. He had commented to his wife that he was an intelligent man, who expressed his opinions well and was interested in bettering himself. He apparently was fairly well off, though Georgiana did not necessarily have to be concerned with that, since she would bring her own fortune to a marriage. Regardless, he was a progressive thinker, as Darcy had noted upon his choice of reading material that morning, something that Elizabeth could only approve of. He seemed to respect and appreciate Georgiana for who she was so far.

Only time would tell if he and Georgiana would make a good match, and Elizabeth wasn't ready to put the cart before the horse. While he and Georgiana had spent a great deal of time conversing in the past two days, and Georgiana seemed more at ease with him than she normally did with strangers, she knew the young woman would not give her heart easily after the debacle of Ramsgate. It was too soon to speculate on what would happen. Now if she could just convince her husband of that.

*****

Georgiana woke to a bright beam of sunlight that peeked through the drawn curtains and fell across her face. A smile crossed her face at the cheery morning sun. They would get to have their picnic after all! She crawled out of bed and made her way over to pull back the drapes with a spring in her step. She flung the fabric away from the window, bathing herself in the morning light, and looked out. The picture the grounds presented was very different from the day before. Servants bustled about, and as she watched, the grooms brought out a pair of horses to two gentlemen, who stood awaiting them. It was difficult to tell from this distance, but she thought it was probably both Mr. Crosbys, going for a ride together. Curious, she watched as they mounted and started off together in the direction of the woods.

As they retreated farther into the distance she refocused her attention on the yard and the gardens beyond. While the grounds were well-manicured, as was expected of a home of the Bingleys, there was a small stream that meandered through with copse of trees on the boundary of the gardens. The spot looked particularly inviting to Georgiana, as it reminded her of her special retreat at home.

With the idea planted, she quickly rang for her maid to get ready for the day. A short time later, she made her way from the house toward the isolated spot.

Her pale, pistachio green dress billowed in the breeze and the sun glinted off her simple up-do, creating the illusion of a halo around her head. In her hand she held a leather-bound journal and a charcoal pencil.

She picked her way along the precise paths to the stream, where a trail broke off to the right. It meandered for a short distance before she found herself sheltered among the trees she had admired from her window. A small wooden bench was situated below the largest oak tree, with the stream only about a meter away.

She glanced longingly at the cool water but made her way to the bench with a sigh. She couldn't very well explain away the dirt and grass stains on her dress, even if the water did entice her. While she could have gotten away with it at Pemberley (her maids were very experienced at removing such stains and very discreet), she had no desire to be caught in such a state by Caroline or one of the gentlemen.

Settling on the bench, she flipped through pages filled with neat, even handwriting and pencil sketches to a fresh page in her journal. The crisp, white page beckoned to her, begging to be filled with her thoughts and feelings. Having neglected her journal for two days now, she eagerly fell to writing.

A lot had occurred in two days, she thought ruefully, looking over what she had written. She had filled several pages already and there was still much to tell. She was glad to have the opportunity to put pencil to paper and work out how she was feeling about everything that had gone on. It wasn't everyday that she went head-to-head with Caroline, learned her niece wanted to become a pirate, and met an interesting young man.

When her words had exhausted themselves, she sat back and reviewed the pages before her. For any young lady of gentle breeding it would have been an intense and overwhelming few days, but Georgiana found herself strangely exhilarated by it all. She hadn't felt so alive in a long time.

Feeling bold and a little indecorous, she flipped to a new page and again put her pencil to paper, this time in the creation of a sketch. Beneath her deft fingers a portrait quickly emerged. Jovial, almond eyes soon twinkled out at the viewer, followed swiftly by an aquiline nose, and full, bow-shaped lips. A strong chin and square jaw line framed in the features and a mess of curly hair topped off the likeness.

She frowned down at the portrait. Something was not quite right. She erased a few strokes and redrew the mouth, the corners curving into a smile. She nodded; that was better. A well-drawn rendering of Thaddeus Crosby stared back at her from the page.

*****

Thaddeus strode purposefully toward the house, leading his horse, frustration radiating from his every pore. His horse had thrown a shoe, cutting his cathartic morning ride short. He trudged along the banks of the small stream, hoping that the soothing waters would help to calm his nerves for the day ahead. As he neared the house, he entered a small copse of trees, and noticed Georgiana seated on the bench. He unconsciously slowed to observe her.

She was wearing another simple yet elegant gown, this one in a pale green that was particularly befitting in the natural setting. She was illuminated by a shaft of light streaming through the branches above her. It reflected off her blonde hair, creating a halo of light around her head. She appeared to be reading, looking down at a volume she held in her hand.

He was drawn to her serenity. She still hadn't noticed him approaching. Feeling somewhat guilty for not making himself known already, he called out, "Good morning, Miss Darcy! Are you enjoying the fine weather today?"

Startled, she snapped the tome in her hand shut as her head jerked up and her eyes flew to meet his. After a moment's pause, she responded, "Good morning to you as well, Mr. Crosby. I was glad to be able to escape the house, as you evidently were, too." She gestured at the horse he was leading. "Did you enjoy your ride?"

"For as long as it lasted," he said, with a rueful smile. "My horse threw a shoe. I'm on my way back to the stables now."

"I'm headed back as well," she responded. "It should be just about time for breakfast."

"May I walk with you?" he asked. "Since we are both headed in that direction." She quickly acquiesced and rose to join him. They started back towards the house, the horse following placidly behind them.

"What were you reading?" Thaddeus inquired curiously, gesturing to the volume in her hand.

Georgiana tightened her grip on the journal as she responded stiffly, "I wasn't reading. This is my journal." Thaddeus looked at her strangely, surprised at her tone. She took a moment to soften her manner before she added, "Do you think we'll be able to have our picnic today since the weather is so fine?"

"I would think so," Thaddeus responded. "I'm sure everyone is eager to enjoy some time outside after being cooped up in the house all day yesterday."

"Most of us are, I think," Georgiana said, thinking of Caroline. She had never been much of an outdoorswoman, even when she had been pursuing Darcy, who was known for his love of nature.

Thaddeus glanced at Georgiana with a smile. She blushed, realizing he had understood her train of thought.

"I'm sure no one will want to be left out," he responded. This was doubtless true, for Caroline was not one to watch from the sidelines when she could be the center of attention. She would want to be included in any group activity.

"Thea and Geoffrey will enjoy the chance to be with everyone," Georgiana commented.

"Yes," Thaddeus said. "I'm sure they will love to be able to run around without being under their nurse's thumb. I know I relished the opportunity when I was a child."

Georgiana smiled at the image of Thaddeus as a young child. "I think you must have been a very mischievous little boy. You must have gotten into a lot of scrapes as a child."

Thaddeus winked. "Not that anyone can prove. Although, I'm sure my brother might try to convince you otherwise."

She laughed and asked him to elaborate. He did and the time passed quickly. They soon neared the house, and Georgiana broke off to continue inside. Thaddeus continued to the stable to hand off his horse and head back into the house, a spring in his step and a jaunty tune upon his lips.

*****

Later that day, the promised picnic came to fruition. The servants set up a canopy for them to lounge under on the front lawn. The bright sunshine filtered through the white cotton, creating a kind of haziness. A few of the guests already lounged with lazy boredom among the cushions and blankets. Caroline, as Thaddeus had expected, was not to be left out. She was propped up, fanning herself indolently and looking bored. Her husband sat a short distance away, fiddling idly with his pocket watch. Thaddeus sprawled next to his brother, fidgeting impatiently and watching the house.

"Alfred," Caroline commanded, "do bring me a glass of sherry, dear." Mr. Crosby got up to get her drink and was returning to her when the door of the house opened, and more of their party emerged to join them.

Thaddeus immediately straightened, but tried to look uninterested in those joining them. Mr. Crosby watched his brother with no small amount of amusement. He leaned over to whisper in his wife's ear as he handed her the sherry, "I think my brother is a little enamored of Georgiana Darcy. See how he is pretending not to notice her? Rather reminds me of our early days."

Caroline gave him a fond smile and turned to watch her brother-in-law, who appeared to be intently studying a grasshopper while sneaking glances at the group making their way over. Thaddeus looked up at them suddenly and caught them watching him. He scowled, which only resulted in the couple breaking out into twin smiles.

"I see what you mean," Caroline murmured, her boredom forgotten. "This is becoming quite an interesting visit." Her hawk-like eyes missed nothing as the Darcys and the Bingleys joined them beneath the canopy. She noticed the glances the two young people sent each other's way when they thought no one was looking. She saw Thaddeus' attentiveness to Georgiana, even while he endeavored to remain in impassive. She saw the pink spring up into the young woman's cheeks when she met Thaddeus' eyes, and she observed the ease of their conversation.

Caroline, although past her own designs on the Mr. Darcy, nevertheless found this new turn of events to be very promising. If she dwelled a little more than necessary of the possibility of her social status being helped along by closer ties to the illustrious Darcys, well, it must be acknowledged that we all have our faults.

Soon after the other adults had joined the fellow guests on the lawn, the children were brought out by their nurse. Elizabeth rose to take her son from the nurse, while Thea went to sit on her aunt's lap. Darcy leaned over to tickle Will as Elizabeth sat back down next to him. Geoffrey made quick work of greeting his parents before joining his cousin next to Georgiana. He seemed to really enjoy having someone his own age to play with.

"Hello, Geoffrey," Georgiana greeted him. "What have you and Thea been up to today?"

The young man responded a little sullenly, "Nurse made us stay inside and play quietly this morning since we were havin' a picnic. We couldn't even leave the nursery. She just wanted to read us stories."

"Did you enjoy the stories, Thea?" Georgiana asked the little girl.

"They were okay," she responded, "but I like the stories Mama reads to me better." Georgiana wasn't surprised. Since both Thea's parents were well-read, they were grooming their daughter to follow in their footsteps. It was a common occurrence to find her niece on her mother or father's lap, a book in hand.

"They weren't even excitin'," Geoffrey complained, breaking into Georgiana's thoughts. "They were all about 'good little boys and girls.'"

Georgiana had to hide her smile. Obviously the subliminal messages his parents had been trying to send hadn't found a receptive audience.

Thaddeus had managed to work his way over to a seat near Georgiana during the confusion of everyone arriving.

"Perhaps you could ask to choose a different book next time," he suggested.

"Maybe," Geoffrey grumbled, "but Nurse doesn't let me inta the libry to pick different ones. She says I might destroy 'em."

Georgiana smothered her mirth. She never could figure out how Thaddeus managed to remain so serious while conversing with the children, but she appreciated the effort. She knew his mien made Geoffrey and Thea feel like their thoughts and feelings were important, too. There were many adults who would dismiss their concerns as insignificant.

"Well, if you're careful with your other toys, then Nurse might think you're big enough to play with the books from the library," Thaddeus responded. Geoffrey harrumphed, but made no further attempts to defend himself. Thea on the other hand, had no such compunction.

"That's what I told him," she declared. "He's always breakin' his toys. I never break my toys. I'm careful." She sent a smug look at Geoffrey, who scowled.

"Yes, dear," Georgiana said, trying to soothe some hurt feelings. "But I'm sure Geoffrey does his best to take care of his toys, too." Thea looked like she didn't believe that for a second, but she wisely held her tongue when her aunt shot her a warning look.

"Now that you are outside, would you like to go for a walk along the stream?" Georgiana offered, distracting the children from the subject at hand.

The suggestion was eagerly taken up by Thea and Geoffrey, and after their parents quickly agreed to the idea, they set off for the stream, Thaddeus and Georgiana in tow. The adults allowed the children to run ahead, keeping them in sight but following a little more sedately behind them.

"So, Miss Darcy, have you enjoyed your picnic so far?" Thaddeus asked, trying to draw her out.

"I have," she assented, "although it has only just begun. I can't help but enjoy any time I get to spend with my family, especially my niece and nephew."

Thaddeus peeked over at her and noticed the wistful, faraway look she sent after her niece. Curious he asked, "Are you anticipating being separated from them soon?"

Surprised at his perceptiveness, Georgiana paused, before answering honestly, "Someday, I hope to have a home of my own. I am not so naïve to be unaware that the probability of settling near my family is not very high. I need to take advantage of the time I have with them."

Unconsciously, she had tightened her grip on his arm as she spoke. Feeling a bit awed by her candidness with him, Thaddeus reached over and covered her hand with his own. She glanced at their hands in surprise, then back up at his face. She met his eyes and their gazes held for a long moment before she turned away shyly, looking back at the children ahead of them. But she didn't remove her hand from his arm and buoyed by this, Thaddeus left his hand covering hers as they walked.

The couple fell into a companionable silence as they made their way to join the children at the side of the stream. Geoffrey was pointing out something to Thea in the reeds as they reached them.

"What did you find?" Georgiana asked, finally pulling away to peer into the water.

"It's a frog," Thea remarked matter-of-factly. "See, it's green and slimy and everything."

Georgiana leaned in a little further. "I see that."

Without warning, the frog jumped directly at them. Thea screamed, and she and Geoffrey both leaped back into Georgiana, knocking her off balance. Thaddeus watched as in seemingly slow motion she toppled into the stream. He moved quickly, attempting to catch her, but it was too late. She landed with a loud splash on her derrière, sputtering.

"Are you all right, Miss Darcy?" he asked worriedly, wading in, heedless of his own clothing, to fish her out.

She accepted the hand he held out to her. "I am, Mr. Crosby. Just, a little, umm, wet." He helped her back up onto the shoreline. He took pity on her and offered his jacket to cover her dripping form, although he had to admit to himself that her clinging wet gown revealed a very pleasant figure.

Georgiana gratefully accepted the jacket, wrapping it around herself modestly. For the first time, she noticed his wet boots and breeches. She paled at the sight, for they were surely ruined. She looked back up at his face. He didn't seem angry, but she knew the items were no doubt costly. If anything, he actually seemed to be amused by the incident, now that he knew she was all right. She lowered her gaze, embarrassed and a little afraid he would still become upset with her, and suggested they head back to the house, since they were both in need of a change of clothes.

The children followed meekly, a little intimidated by the unintentional mischief they had made.

Elizabeth was the first to notice them approaching, and not immediately recognizing the state they were in, called out, "You are back soon! Were there no birds to look at?"

The foursome drew closer, and Elizabeth's eyes widened as she realized her sister was drenched. But it was Caroline who spoke first.

"Good Lord, did you fall in Miss Darcy? How quaint!" She snickered. A glare from her husband quickly silenced her, quelling her humor.

Georgiana tried to ignore the comment, although Thaddeus, standing beside her, could not help but notice her stiffening.

"I am afraid I did," she said with a small smile.

Elizabeth immediately got to her feet, and wrapping one arm around her, she quickly drew her away towards the house. "Come, let's get you into some dry clothes." Georgiana gratefully leaned into her. Elizabeth met her husband's eyes over her sister's head and he responded quickly to her silent message, taking the two children in hand as she went with Georgiana.

As they walked away, Caroline turned back to the group, mindless of the company, and said, "Did you see her hem? Six inches deep in mud!"

She suddenly realized that no one else found the situation quite so outrageous. Even Thaddeus, who was wont to laugh at anything, was glaring at her. She looked around at all the serious faces and quickly suppressed whatever she had been about to say next.

Silence reigned for a few moments before Thaddeus excused himself to change. Jane, ever the peacemaker, changed the subject, carrying the stilted conversation until Thaddeus rejoined the group.

*****

Caroline's comment filtered to Georgiana and Elizabeth's ears as they walked away. "Did you see her hem? Six inches deep in mud!"

Elizabeth tightened her hold on her sister as she almost tripped. Georgiana, already embarrassed, and shy by nature, was mortified. She blushed, and made the rest of the trip into the house silent, with her eyes downcast.

Once inside her room, Elizabeth handed Georgiana over to the capable hands of her maid.

"I'll just be in the drawing room if you need anything," she informed her sister, hesitant to leave her.

Georgiana nodded and smiled reassuringly but Elizabeth just threw her a skeptical look as she reluctantly went out the door.

"Oh, Miss, you are soaked through! Let's get you out of those wet clothes and into a hot bath. Don't want you to go and get a cold now, do we?" Her maid fussed over her, clucking over the state of her clothes.

Georgiana submitted to her ministrations meekly. Far too meekly, her maid felt, as she was used to a much livelier mistress. Her harrumphs, however, were ignored by her mistress, who was too wrapped up in her own thoughts to notice. Despite her attempts to express her indignation, the maid eventually was forced to leave Georgiana to relax in her bath.

She dragged her fingers idly through the sudsy waters, then groaned and threw her head back against the rim of the tub. *How could I be so clumsy!* she thought.

Her cheeks bright even in the privacy of her own room, she remembered Mrs. Crosby's comments:

"Good Lord, did you fall in Miss Darcy? How quaint!" Caroline snickered.

Georgiana felt like a little girl all over again. Caroline's laughing eyes seemed to mock her from the depths of the tub. *And in front of Mr. Crosby, too! What he must think of me!* After that episode he surely wouldn't view her as the refined, elegant young woman she wanted him to see. No, she was just a bumbling idiot, who managed to make a fool of herself wherever she went. She put one hand up to her brow, covering her face in shame. There was no way she could join them now. She just wanted to sink down in the water and disappear. What a fool she must look!

Like any young woman of good breeding, though, Georgiana knew she could not remain in the bath forever. She would have to face reality sooner or later, and it was not worth procrastinating. She would handle the situation with all the poise and maturity she had, as any woman of her station should. *Nay, as a Darcy should!*

Albeit reluctantly, she called for her maid and climbed out of the tub with determination. She would make her ancestors proud, even if inwardly she was quaking in her slippers. She would not disappoint.

Georgiana prepared herself to return to company with the single-mindedness of one preparing for battle. She armed herself with an azure gown that drew attention to her porcelain skin and a simple, elegant up-do that brought the focus to her eyes.

Those same eyes, which instantly lightened to reflect the blue of her new gown, swept over her reflection critically, looking for any chinks in her armor. Satisfied that there were none, she put her Darcy mask firmly in place. In the mirror, she was the very picture of a fashionable, elegant, proud member of the tonnage. Only if you looked very closely, deep into her eyes, could you see the insecure, bashful young woman who was the real Georgiana.

Elizabeth recognized the Darcy mask in place when Georgiana came to join her in the drawing room, but chose not to remark on it. She had seen it in place too often on both her husband and his sister to comment on it now. It was unlikely to do any harm under the circumstances, and would offer Georgiana some protection from Caroline's stinging comments.

"Are you ready to rejoin the picnic?" Elizabeth asked.

Georgiana raised her chin an inch, and her eyes steeled, but Elizabeth, knowing what was behind the mask, was not intimidated.

"I am," Georgiana asserted, her voice cool and aloof. "We've kept them waiting long enough, I suppose."

Elizabeth's eyes twinkled merrily at her sister. "Oh dear, Georgiana, I'm afraid that sounded an awful lot like something Caroline would say."

Georgiana look horrified. "Oh, I'm so sorry Elizabeth! Please forgive me! You know I don't mean to be rude."

"I know, dear," Elizabeth reassured her, "but perhaps you should soften the mask a little around the edges. You wouldn't want to give the wrong idea to anyone here."

Georgiana looked a little ashamed. "You're right. I'll try." Elizabeth patted her hand, and she took a couple of moments to recompose herself before they headed out to the picnic.

*****

Thaddeus had returned to the picnic long before the women arrived. He had only had to change his boots and breeches to be presentable for company once again. He sat, fidgeting, listening to the conversation going on around him but not participating in it. He was not the only one. He noticed Darcy was also abstaining from joining in the festivities. Instead, the older man was alternating between entertaining his children and watching Thaddeus intently.

It was a little disconcerting, to tell the truth. Thaddeus met Darcy's eyes, not willing to let himself be intimidated. The older man met his gaze for a long moment, neither of them moving or looking away. Then, as if reaching an inner decision, Darcy rose to join him, bringing his son with him. Thea was a little startled by her father's sudden absconding, and the shy little girl quickly looked around for a replacement, but with her mother and aunt out of the picture, there was no one else for her to hide behind. Somewhat reluctantly, she followed her father, skirting the edges of the company to take a seat beside him.

Geoffrey gestured for her to come and sit by him, but after the trouble they had caused already, Thea didn't want to run the risk of a repeat. She was going to err on the side of caution and stick by her father. She shook her head and stuck out her tongue at him.

Darcy shot her a reprimanding glance before turning to Thaddeus.

"Crosby, I…" he started to say, an intense look on his face.

"MR. DARCY!" Darcy's head swung around violently as his wife's voice rang out across the yard. She hurried to reach his side. "Mr. Darcy, I was just telling Georgiana I needed to consult with you about something." She tugged him away from Thaddeus, the irritation evident on his face. Georgiana, who had followed her sister at a more sedate pace, smiled shyly at Thaddeus before hurrying off after the Darcys.

Thaddeus couldn't help but be amused by the interchange between husband and wife. It was obvious that Mrs. Darcy had purposefully intervened to keep her husband from expressing something he might later regret. He was fairly certain what Darcy wanted to talk to him about. He *had* shown a lot of interest in Georgiana in the last few days and Darcy was not the type of man to beat about the bush. Now, the real question was, how would he have answered the question?

Unfortunately, a picnic was not the place for such introspection, and Thaddeus was torn from his thoughts by a small voice at his side and a tug on his coat sleeve.

"Mr. Crosby?" Thea's face peered up at him worriedly. "Do you think Aunt Georgiana is mad at us for pushing her in the river?"

"I don't think she is. But I don't know her as well as you do, Miss Darcy. Does she look mad to you?" Thaddeus asked.

The little girl glanced across the tent at her aunt before turning back. "No. I don't think so. But she *does* look like Papa does when he's upset or embarrassed about something but doesn't want anyone else to know."

Thaddeus turned to take a second look at Georgiana, and was impressed with the little girl's discernment. To an ordinary viewer, Georgiana carried herself much as she normally would, if a little stiffer. He would never have noticed the difference if Thea hadn't pointed it out to him, much less understood the reason behind it.

He turned his attention back to Thea. "You're probably right, Miss Darcy. Do you think if you went over there and gave her a hug that would make her feel better?"

The girl considered his suggestion seriously, observing her aunt before acquiescing. Thaddeus watched as she made her way over to the older woman.

Thea tugged on Georgiana's skirts, her thumb in her mouth. Thaddeus could see the confused look on Georgiana's face as she turned to face the little girl. She crouched down, lowering herself to the child's level to listen to whatever Thea was saying. Her face softened as Thea wound her arms around her neck.

Thaddeus' throat constricted as he watched Georgiana squeeze Thea back. He could almost feel the relief and comfort that simple hug offered to her. Briefly, as she held Thea, he felt like he could see straight into the depths of her being. Here was a woman who valued family above all else. Occasionally, she chose to hide how she was feeling from those undeserving, but she had been remarkably magnanimous with him, allowing him to glimpse the true woman underneath society's strictures. She was gentle, kind, considerate, with a gift for music and a love for children.

His heart warmed a little more toward her, watching her interact with her niece.

He turned away from the scene in front of him before Georgiana could look up and catch him staring. Feeling a little lost, he sought out his brother for some inane conversation, later realizing he had no recollection of what they had spoken of.

*****

The company, worn out physically and emotionally after the long afternoon outdoors, retired early that night. Georgiana was glad for the reprieve from company. For her introverted personality, the last few days with their social demands had been exhausting. Even with the time she had sought out for herself, it was wearing on her.

Alone in her room, she curled up on the settee clad in her nightdress, taking time just to enjoy the privacy. There were no demands on her time now, no one to impress, no conversations to be a part of. She could just *be*.

A single candle was lit on the side table, casting soft shadows about the room. Georgiana caressed the cover of the book in front of her. She wasn't ready yet to delve into its pages and glimpse another world and another time. She wanted to savor the moment. She set aside the book and rose to gaze out the window.

She laid one hand gently against the pane and peered up at the stars. She took her time admiring them, awed by the grandeur of the night sky and her own insignificance in the grand scheme of things. For the moment, her problems seemed small and far away. She turned back into the room, able to find peace, for the time at least. She picked up the book and candle holder and set them on her nightstand before climbing into bed. At least this night sleep would come easily.

*****

Elizabeth Darcy was in the midst of berating her husband as her sister-in-law was admiring the starry sky.

"What were you thinking?! Can you imagine how embarrassed Georgiana would be?! She's already had a rough day with Caroline making those horrid comments. How would she feel if she realized you were about to interrogate Mr. Crosby about her?!" Elizabeth paced the room, speaking furiously in hushed tones in order to avoid being overheard by the household. Her husband sat on a bench at the end of the bed, pulling off his boots.

He sighed. "I know, dear." He tugged fruitlessly on his boot, waiting for his wife's ire to be spent. Finally, he asked, "Will you help me with this?"

She stormed over and pulled hard on the boot, distractedly putting her entire weight into it. Briefly, it looked like the boot might win, but suddenly it released, sending Elizabeth onto the floor, a stunned look on her face.

For a moment, Elizabeth and Darcy were startled into silence, but then their eyes met and they both burst out laughing, the tension dissipating. Darcy held out a hand to help his wife up onto the bench beside him.

"I'm sorry, Will. I just didn't want Georgiana to be upset any further. You should have seen her when we came back to the house to change. She was mortified! I know you wouldn't do anything to hurt her on purpose, but sometimes I don't think you realize how your actions affect her. Will you forgive me for being so churlish?" Elizabeth repented.

Darcy wrapped his arm around his wife's shoulders and pulled her against his side. "You know I will." He relented and admitted ruefully, "You were right to think I didn't really consider how Georgiana would feel about my approaching Mr. Crosby. I guess I just got caught up. I'll try to keep my protective instincts under control."

Darcy smiled down at his wife, and she snuggled closer to his side, sighing. Having forgiven and being forgave, the couple turned in for the night.

*****

Meanwhile, down the hall, Caroline and Alfred Crosby were having a discussion of their own.

The door between their rooms open, Alfred paused in the doorway, tugging off his cravat. "Your comments about Miss Darcy this afternoon were a little uncalled for, don't you think?"

Caroline paused in brushing out her hair and turned to face her husband. "What? I hardly said anything. Surely no one minded. Besides, did you *see* her hem?" she asked incredulously.

"Yes, I saw her hem," Alfred said, irritated, "but I also didn't think it was as funny as you seemed to. I thought it was quite rude, and Miss Darcy was certainly mortified."

Caroline turned back to the mirror and began brushing her hair to cover her discomfiture. Feigning a nonchalant attitude, she said, "Well, I don't think she heard me anyway."

Alfred, knowing his wife and seeing the regret she was trying to hide, crossed the room to join her at the vanity. He tenderly grasped her chin and turned her head to face him. He waited until she met his eyes.

"She heard you," he informed her gently. She looked away, unable to meet his eyes.

"Are you going to apologize?" he asked, hopeful. He knew it would be a humbling experience, but Caroline was no shrinking violet. He was confident she would do the right thing, as much against her nature as it was.

She sighed, and said grudgingly, "I'll apologize." She returned to brushing her hair. "But don't expect me to be happy about it." Alfred smiled as he went back through the door into his own chamber. That was his Caroline.

*****

Jane Bingley crawled into bed beside her husband and allowed Charles to cradle her against his side. She was still early on enough in her pregnancy that her body easily molded into his. He laid a hand tenderly on her slightly expanded stomach and caressed the delicate flesh through her nightdress.

"How are you my dear?" he asked considerately. "Is the company too much for you?"

Jane sighed and laid her head on his shoulder. "No. It is exhausting, but I tire more easily now anyway." She glanced up at him with a smile. "It is such a joy to have Lizzy here. You can't imagine how much it means to me to get to share this time with her. I have missed her so much. And Geoffrey actually seems to be behaving himself with Thea in residence." She paused and they shared a wry smile at the thought of their firstborn. "At least for the most part."

*****

For his part, Thaddeus was also gazing out the window, but he wasn't observing the night sky as Georgiana had done. He was lost in introspection. His mind was back on the would-have-been discussion that afternoon with Mr. Darcy. How would he have answered if Mr. Darcy had asked his question?

Was he interested in Georgiana Darcy as a wife?

Chapter 6

A fortnight later, Georgiana Darcy found herself ensconced in the library, enjoying the relative quiet of the morning. The only sounds that reached her ears were the quiet pitter-patter of feet as the maids and footmen passed the double doors into the library. She was curled up on the window seat, as had become her habit. The window seat and the bench by the stream had quickly become her favorite places in Chetborn. For the most part, anyone seeking her before breakfast could find her at one of the two places.

Comfortable that she would not be disturbed, she had kicked off her slippers and pulled her feet up on the seat. She leaned back against the bookshelf that framed the seat, resting her book on her drawn up knees, and looked out the window at the busy scene below. Maids, footmen, grooms, and stable boys hurried below on unknown errands. The head gardener and his underlings were busy at work, trimming and pruning. Georgiana took a moment to admire their handiwork, although it was a little too manicured for her taste.

A noise from the doorway drew her attention and she turned to look. She smiled at Thaddeus standing in the entrance.

Thaddeus, once again caught in the act of admiring her, walked further into the room. The morning sun streaming through the window bathed Georgiana in a warm glow. Her welcoming smile beckoned him as she sat up and modestly slid her feet back into her slippers.

"Have you come in search of a book, Mr. Crosby?" Georgiana asked good-naturedly.

"No, I've come to return one," Thaddeus said, holding up the book in his hand, which lent credibility to his presence in the library. "I've had a letter from my man of business so I thought to return this before I left for town on the morrow."

"Oh," Georgiana said, trying to hide her disappointment. "Will you be returning after you've finished your business?"

"It depends. I am at my brother's disposal. If he remains here, in the country, then I'll be back," Thaddeus replied. "I do hope I'll be able to return, though. I've thoroughly enjoyed my stay here."

He smiled gently, hoping that it would soften the blow that he was leaving. The past two weeks in constant company with each other had proven that there was some connection between them. He was loath to leave with things unspoken between them, but his business was urgent and he could put it off no longer. He sincerely hoped that his brother would remain at Chetborn a while longer, but with no idea of the duration of his stay in town, he didn't want to give her false hope. He would find a way to see her again, somehow, even if Alfred did return to his own estate, Aysthorpe Hall.

She returned his smile as best as she could, but he could tell she was holding back and trying to hide what she truly thought and felt.

"I do hope you are able to conclude your business to your satisfaction," she said politely, gripping her book in one hand a little tighter than necessary.

Thaddeus made his way to one of the bookshelves and returned the tome to its place. Turning back to Georgiana, he said, "I think it will be, and hopefully, it will come to a speedy conclusion as well."

This time, her smile was genuine as it reached her eyes. The light in her eyes at his insinuation warmed his heart. He offered her his arm, feeling inordinately pleased with himself, and she rose gracefully to accept it as he asked her, "It is just about time to break our fast; may I have the pleasure of accompanying you to the breakfast room?"

They made their way to the breakfast room slowly, both aware of the impending separation, but determined to make the most of the few hours they had left together. They still reached the room with time to spare before any of the others could be expected to make an appearance.

Thaddeus filled both of their plates while Georgiana poured them coffee. They split the morning paper, and fell to reading while they ate, enjoying the companionable silence. Thaddeus imagined spending every morning this way, a thought that wouldn't have crossed his stubborn bachelor mind a month earlier.

Eventually, their solitude was broken when Mr. and Mrs. Darcy joined them at the table. By this time, Thaddeus was finished with the paper and gamely offered his portion to Darcy, who was eyeing it eagerly. He knew better by now than to try to involve either Georgiana or Darcy in conversation while they were reading, so he turned his attention to Elizabeth.

"How are you doing this morning, Mrs. Darcy?" he asked politely. "Are you enjoying the sunshine?"

Elizabeth smiled, always glad to have someone to converse with at the breakfast table, and responded, "Isn't it so pleasant to wake up to the sunshine? These last few days of rain have been so dull."

"I do enjoy the sunshine, especially while I'm in the country. It's hard to appreciate a sunny day while you're in town with all the smog and heat," Thaddeus replied.

Elizabeth wrinkled her nose. "Yes, I find town distasteful, especially in summer. I try to avoid it as much as possible."

Thaddeus sighed. "I wish I could avoid it. Unfortunately, I'm to travel there on the morrow to attend to some business. I'll just have to suffer with the rest of the fellows I suppose."

Elizabeth paused in slicing her cold cuts and looked up at him in surprise. "You're traveling to town tomorrow?"

He sipped from his coffee cup before replying, "I am. I received some correspondence from my man of business yesterday and there are a few matters that require my personal attention. I hope to only be gone for a few days, but there is no way of knowing how long my attendance will be necessary."

Elizabeth contemplated him as he returned to his meal. Thaddeus tried to ignore her unnerving gaze, but he was very aware of the scrutiny he was under.

Finally, Elizabeth returned to her meal and Thaddeus breathed a sigh of relief.

"You must be disappointed to be called away at such a time," Elizabeth commented nonchalantly.

Thaddeus almost choked on his food, swallowing hard. He should have known better, he reflected ruefully. Mrs. Darcy was known for her cutting wit and keen observations, and she wasn't afraid to speak what was on her mind.

He smiled inwardly; she had been a good influence on Georgiana in that regard. His gaze drifted to the woman of his thoughts, who was still absorbed in the paper, and he turned back to his conversation, surprised by his ability to answer calmly. "Yes, I certainly find myself disappointed."

Elizabeth eyed him knowingly, not missing the glance in Georgiana's direction, but only replied, "I see."

Elizabeth caught the sly glance her husband sent her across the table and had to stop herself from laughing. He was not quite as absorbed in his paper as he seemed, but he was keenly interested in where the conversation was leading. She continued to eat silently for a time, collecting herself. Then, when an opening presented itself, she took the opportunity to shift the subject, gleefully thwarting her husband's wishes. Thaddeus gladly followed her lead, despite his ignorance of Mr. Darcy's attention.

Later, the entire group gathered in the drawing room, ostensibly to receive callers, but as none were expected, the reason quickly became social. Georgiana, never much one for gossip, quickly availed herself of the pianoforte off to one side of the room.

As she began to play, Thaddeus quickly followed, using the excuse that she would need someone to turn the pages for her. Georgiana smiled to herself, and caught Elizabeth's amused glance, but did not correct him. She knew the piece she was playing by heart. Indeed, the sheet music on the stand was not even the same piece as what she was playing, but she wouldn't turn down the opportunity for some more intimate conversation.

"You play beautifully," Thaddeus complimented her.

"So you've told me," Georgiana responded archly, one eyebrow raised playfully.

"Have I?" Thaddeus teased. "Shall I compliment the instrument then? Or perhaps the musician?"

Georgiana blushed. "Perhaps you should admire the piece instead."

"Indeed, perhaps I shall," Thaddeus said, leaning in to turn a page at her nod and looking at the music on the stand. He raised an eyebrow. "Hmmm... It appears that I should be complimenting Beethoven on his achievements, but I believe you are playing Mozart instead."

"You have a keen ear, Mr. Crosby," Georgiana demurred, a twinkle in her eye.

"I don't suppose you really need my services as a page turner, then," Thaddeus said, a little disappointed.

"Unless I am playing a new piece, I very rarely require assistance," Georgiana admitted, but went on to reassure him, "but you do me a great service just by keeping me company."

Slightly mollified, Thaddeus replied, "Then I shan't deny you my presence. Do you know a great many pieces then, or just a few choice favorites you prefer to play?"

She paused thoughtfully, even as her hands carried on of their own volition. "I have my favorites that I am comfortable playing around others. But music stays with me as nothing else does. Often I have only to play a piece once or twice before it just seems to flow from my fingertips with little effort."

"Does it speak to you then?" Thaddeus inquired curiously.

"I suppose you could say that," Georgiana said, "although I do not claim to know what the composer was trying to impart. I can only remark on how I feel when I play it and the atmosphere I feel it imparts."

Thaddeus appreciated her modesty, even if it was unwarranted. There were far too many women who would claim a depth of knowledge of music that they did not possess.

"You know what I would like to hear you play..." Thaddeus said, naming the piece. "You always look so joyful when you play that piece."

Georgiana looked a little embarrassed, and objected, "I'm afraid that composition would not really appeal to the company." But she still easily segued into it, to his pleasure.

She watched the company briefly, but no one seemed to notice the change in background music.

"Shall we speak of something besides music?" Thaddeus suggested. "Tell me, Miss Darcy, do you intend to spend the season in town?"

Georgiana stumbled over a few notes in her surprise, and Elizabeth looked up at the discordant sound; but she quickly went back to her conversation at Georgiana's reassuring smile. Turning back to her own conversation, Georgiana frowned slightly, taken aback by the introduction of a dreaded event that wouldn't take place for months yet.

Cautiously, she responded, "At the moment, I do not know. I had intended to attempt to convince my brother to remain at Pemberley, as such occasions do not appeal to me. But he has insisted that we attend every year since I came out. In the end, he will make the decision."

"Perhaps we shall see each other there," Thaddeus said, making the reason behind his question suddenly clear. "I do not often make it up to the Lake District, but I shall be in town for the season." He smiled wryly. "My brother and his wife are always in attendance and for the time at least, I am at his disposal."

Georgiana smiled softly, dismissing any thoughts of convincing her brother to stay at Pemberley and firmly pushing any lingering memories of her previous disastrous seasons to the back of her mind. Maybe she would actually enjoy the season this time around.

"That would be pleasant," Georgiana acknowledged. "It is always good to see one's friends when in town. That is one of the few appeals the country does not have." Shyly, she met his eyes, and volumes were spoken without a word being said.

*****

The day passed much too quickly for the young lovers, as they are oft to when a separation is looming. They spent as much time as they could in each other's company, but in the end, as they knew it must, the time came for them to part ways. They lingered in the drawing room after dinner for as long as they could, but eventually Georgiana could no longer ignore Elizabeth's yawns. Albeit reluctantly, she bid Thaddeus good night and bade him have a safe trip.

Then, with one last backwards glance, she disappeared into the hallway. Now, pacing his room, Thaddeus couldn't help but remember that last glance. He paused at the window to look out, but he quickly grew impatient and returned to his pacing, running his hands through his hair.

Logically, he knew that he needed to go to London to deal with his business, and there was a good chance he would be back before his brother and Caroline decided to move on. But emotionally, he desperately wished he didn't have to go. He wanted to spend every available moment in Georgiana's presence, to bask in her smile, and to laugh with her at Caroline pretensions.

He finally collapsed into bed, worn out emotionally, and fell into a dreamless slumber.

*****

Georgiana woke early the next morning, just as light was beginning to filter over the horizon. She rose and made her way over to the window, wrapping her dressing gown around her. In the gray light of dawn she watched as Thaddeus mounted his horse and rode off down the drive. Just as he reached the summit, before he passed out of sight, he reigned in his horse and turned to take one last look at the grand house behind him.

Georgiana put one hand up to the glass in a silent gesture of farewell. Then, with a flick of his wrist, he crested the hill and was gone. She stood staring after him until the sun was fully over the horizon and the yard was bustling with activity.

*****

In a perfect world, Thaddeus would have returned in three or four days, the couple would have declared their love, become engaged, and lived happily ever after. But this was not a perfect world, and things did not work out quite as they had hoped.

A week later, Thaddeus was finally wrapping up his business matters. Seated across from his man of business, he fidgeted with his pen and inkwell as he listened.

"Now, on to one final matter," the man began to conclude, drawing Thaddeus' wandering attention back. "I've come across an estate for sale I thought you might be interested in. It's in the northern part of the country, so it's being offered at a very reasonable price, well within your budget."

He slid the paperwork across the desk as Thaddeus' hand stilled on the inkwell. After a moment's hesitation, he took up the papers and began to scan them. Inexplicably, the corners of his mouth began to turn up with the hint of a smile, confusing the man across from him.

Thaddeus rubbed his hand across his jaw, tapping one finger on his mouth as he read. Finally, he looked up and said, "Very well. This looks very promising indeed. I should like to see some more information though before I make any decisions."

The man nodded obsequiously. "Right then, sir." A knock sounded at the door to the study, startling the two men, and a servant stuck his head in at Thaddeus' call.

"Begging your pardon, sir," he said, "but the post has arrived."

"Bring it in," Thaddeus commanded, and took the stack of letters. He dismissed the servant and quickly thumbed through them while his man of business sat silently waiting. He had reached the last missive in the pile before he paused and stared at the directions, frowning.

He opened the letter and quickly skimmed through it. With a sigh, he turned back to the patiently waiting man. "You may call on me here when you've gathered the information on that estate. It appears my brother has decided to return to town."

Chapter 7

Elizabeth kept one eye on her children, playing on the library floor in front of the fire, while watching her sister stare out the library windows. The balmy October weather had quickly deteriorated as November approached, trapping them all indoors.

Gray skies and sleet had heralded that November morning, causing them to retreat to one of their favorite rooms in Pemberley. A cheerful fire had lightened the atmosphere, but Georgiana had remained distant. Elizabeth had recognized the familiar retreat to the window for what it was, having often seen her husband resort to the same maneuver in order to avoid conversation.

Darcy was on the floor with Thea and William, trying to keep the little boy from wandering off now that he was crawling. Thea was busy playing with her dolls and repeatedly pouring tea for her parents.

Normally, Elizabeth relished the opportunity for some wholesome family time, especially after having spent so much time away from home and a good part of that time with Caroline Crosby. But today she was distracted by Georgiana. She knew the young woman was disappointed that Thaddeus had been unable to return to Chetborn, and now with their removal to Pemberley and the onset of inclement weather, there would be no opportunity to see him until the spring.

Elizabeth well remembered a time when her separation from Darcy had seemed interminable. She was racking her brain for some way to divert Georgiana when Thea solved the problem for her.

"Auntie, will you come play tea party with me?" Thea asked, crossing the room to lay her small hand in Georgiana's. Georgiana pulled herself from her thoughts and smiled at the little girl in front of her.

"Of course I will, dear," she replied, and allowed herself to be led to her place in front of the fire.

Elizabeth sat back and permitted herself to watch the scene in front of her contentedly.

*****

Winter passed slowly for the separated lovers, as time is bound to do when your heart yearns to be somewhere else. But gradually, the snows melted and the sun returned, and spring arrived in all its glory.

Georgiana eagerly awaited the onset of the season, even as she had initially dreaded it. She marked each sign that the day neared: the crocus peeking through the melting snow, the daffodils merrily bobbing in the wind, even the onslaught of torrential rain that lasted the whole of March, until finally, the day arrived for them to travel to Town.

*****

Georgiana peered eagerly out the carriage windows as they reached the outskirts of Town. Never had London looked so good to her. Somewhere, among the crowds of people, Thaddeus was there too, waiting for her.

Darcy and Elizabeth shared an amused glance at her transparency. They well remembered the early days of their romance, the extended forced separations, and the yearning to see each other once again. Elizabeth was pleased to see her sister come out of her despondency. She hoped that Thaddeus would live up to the favorable impression he had made at Chetborn, and that the couple's shared fondness would become a lasting union.

Darcy had come a long way in accepting that his little sister might actually become someone's wife. Even though he still didn't want to believe that there was any man out there that could be good enough for her, inwardly he had acknowledged that Thaddeus was a good man. He rather liked the chap, even if he didn't want to admit it to his wife.

The trip had been long and arduous and they were all more than ready to disembark when the carriage pulled up in front of the townhome. Darcy was the first out, and he immediately handed out his wife and sister before greeting the housekeeper and butler. Upon entering, they were pleased to find the house aired out and awaiting their arrival.

"It looks as though we never left," Darcy complimented the staff who had gathered to meet them, pulling off his gloves and handing them to a footman.

Elizabeth added, "You've made everything shine so beautifully Mrs. Cole." The housekeeper beamed with pride at the master and mistress' approval.

They shed their outerwear before retiring to their rooms to rest after the long journey. Georgiana was pleased to find a roaring fire burning in her apartments and her lady's maid waiting to help her out of her traveling clothes. She was glad to shed the weighty clothes and wash the dust off, but she was grateful when her maid finally left her alone with her thoughts.

Georgiana repaired to the chaise in her sitting area, reclining with a cup of chocolate the maid had brought. She sipped delicately, allowing the hot beverage to warm her. Thoughtfully, she traced one finger along the brim and sat back with a sigh.

She felt a little on edge, now that the time had finally come. She had spent all winter long hoping and dreaming of what could be. It all hinged on one man, who may, or may not, still be interested in her. It was frightening to have so much riding on someone, and to have no control over the outcome.

Would it be awkward, when they met again? Would he still feel the same way about her? Would he be as handsome as she remembered him? Would he still find her attractive?

There were so many questions, and she had none of the answers. She didn't even know when she would encounter him next. She could only rely on chance to bring them together.

Still the chances were a lot higher, now that they were in the same city. She rose, bringing her mug with her, and crossed to pull back the curtains. Gazing out at the city lights, she could almost feel his presence, near her once again.

*****

Thaddeus stood at the window of his brother's study, swirling his glass of port.

"So you're really thinking of marrying this girl," his brother stated from where he sat behind his desk. He was leaning back in his chair, feet casually propped on the desk top. A smug smirk lingered on his face.

"Yes, Alfred," Thaddeus said long-sufferingly, turning to face his brother briefly. "I'm planning on marrying Georgiana, as you well know."

Alfred, sensing his brother had withstood just about as much mockery as he could stand, lightened his teasing. "I think all your moping and pining this winter impressed that fact upon us all. Caroline even finally noticed something was going on. At the moment she's quite tickled to think you're mooning over some girl."

Thaddeus turned away from the window and joined his brother in a chair on the other side of the desk. "She's not just some girl, Alfred," he said irritably.

"I know," Alfred reassured him, his tone and manners softening. *People in love are so touchy,* he thought. He swirled the port in his glass before taking a swig, and turned back to Thaddeus, suddenly serious. "Can I give you a piece of advice, brother to brother?"

Thaddeus looked up from his own glass, surprised by the sudden change in tone. "I suppose so."

"Take your time to get to know each other," he advised. "I know you feel very strongly about her, but if it's truly love, it can only benefit from some time to mature." He paused before divulging, "As much as I love my wife, there are some things I wish I had known before we were married. Don't make the same mistake I did by rushing into it without really knowing your partner."

Thaddeus could only nod in response. He didn't know how to respond to his brother's intimate disclosure. An uncomfortable silence stretched between them, until finally Thaddeus swallowed the last of his port and stood.

"I think I'll see myself to bed," he announced, which his brother acknowledged with a nod, his eyes glued to his glass of port. Thaddeus stood there awkwardly for a moment, but Alfred seemed lost in his thoughts, so he quietly took himself off to bed with no further comment.

*****

Darcy set off late the next morning for his club, glad to be able to escape the house before the first round of callers. He was not looking forward to the influx of people into his home, eager to gossip after the inactivity of winter, and he suspected that neither his wife nor his sister would enjoy the social demands to come that day. Thankfully, they only received visitors a few days out of the week, so his sanctuary would be restored to him once again on the morrow.

He found the masculine air of White's to be somewhat refreshing after a winter spent surrounded by women. He greeted a few of his acquaintances with a nod before settling into an armchair with the paper and a glass of brandy, projecting his desire for solitude.

There was naught but melted ice in his glass and he was lingering over the last of his paper when someone settled into the chair next to him, drawing his attention. He glanced over, expecting to be annoyed by some overly friendly young buck who couldn't take a hint, when he was pleasantly surprised to recognize the man comfortably ensconced next to him.

"Crosby! What a pleasure to see you here! I didn't know you belonged to White's," Darcy greeted the younger man.

"Yes, well, it's a recent development," Thaddeus commented wryly. "When did you arrive in town?"

"Just yesterday," Darcy answered. "The ladies were expecting visitors today so I thought to make myself scarce. Not my sort of thing."

"No, I dare say it's not any man's," Thaddeus said with humor. The two men shared a smirk.

"Care to have a drink?" Darcy asked, signaling a waiter at Thaddeus' nod. "How did you pass the winter?"

"I spent it here in Town with my brother and his wife." He shared a significant glance with Darcy, who did not envy the young man his accommodations. "My sister prefers to be near her friends so she can still visit and engage in social activities during the little season."

"Ah yes," Darcy remarked, swirling the liquor in his glass. "The joys of seeing and being seen. I hate Town."

Thaddeus laughed. "Then why have you come to Town if you hate it so much?"

Darcy gave him a piercing stare. "I think you know the answer to that as well as I do."

Thaddeus swallowed hard, making no reply. The reason was obvious to them both.

They shared a long, hard look, before Darcy finally let him off the hook.

Setting aside his glass, he asked, "I don't suppose you'd like to come to dinner tonight."

Thaddeus smiled in relief and pleasure. "I'd love too."

*****

Darcy strode purposefully into the townhouse, pulling off his gloves and handing them to a footman. "Have you seen Mrs. Darcy, Smith?"

The footman accepted the gloves. "I believe she's in the drawing room, Mr. Darcy."

"Have her join me in my study, please," he commanded, his voice reiterating that he was every bit the master of the house.

The footman bowed deeply and went to do his bidding. Darcy turned and headed in the direction of the study.

A short time later, his wife knocked gently on the door, poking her head in. "You wanted to see me?"

"Yes," Darcy said, beckoning for her to come in and close the door behind her. "I wanted to let you know we'll be one more for dinner. I've invited Mr. Crosby to join us."

"Mr. Crosby?" Elizabeth exclaimed, taking the seat in front of his desk. "Where did you see him?"

"He was at my club this morning. Sat down right next to me as I was reading the paper," Darcy said, a little wonderingly.

"He dared to interrupt you reading?" Elizabeth teased.

"Yes," Darcy said gruffly, unsure how to respond to her mockery.

Elizabeth took pity on her husband, offering him an olive branch by saying, "Georgiana will be excited to see him, especially so soon after arriving in Town. Should we tell her we're expecting him for dinner?"

"No, just tell her we're expecting company. There's no way of knowing how he feels about her after such a long separation. I don't want her to get her hopes up," Darcy told his wife.

Elizabeth agreed to keep the secret, getting up from her seat. "I'd best let Mrs. Cole know we're expecting one more for dinner and make sure that the menu is suitable for company." She came around the desk to give her husband a peck on the cheek before exiting.

Darcy watched his wife leave, and then turned back to the paperwork in front of him. There was no use worrying about the night before them yet. He had more pressing matters to deal with at the moment, namely how he was going to weasel out of the fitting his wife had planned for him at the tailor's.

*****

Thaddeus arrived exactly on time to the Darcy's London home. He was a little over-awed by the grand home as he stepped out of his carriage. He squelched the urge to tug on his cravat as he uncomfortably mounted the steps. He knew the Darcys were wealthy and influential members of the Ton, but it humbled him to see the grandeur in which they lived. His family was considered well off by any means, and he generally could afford whatever luxuries he desired, but he suddenly felt quite in over his head.

These people had more money than he had ever dreamed of, and Georgiana had been raised among this wealth and splendor. How could she ever consider him, a younger son, with only five thousand pounds a year to his name, as a suitable husband?

Still, he reminded himself as he was admitted into the hall and directed to the parlor, *these are my friends*. They certainly hadn't seemed to look down on him at Chetborn. The Darcys were by no means pretentious. The rooms he was passing through were tastefully decorated, stylish without being ostentatious. He had nothing to worry about. Darcy wouldn't have invited him for dinner if he didn't consider him a serious candidate for his sister's hand. He was not a man to act idly.

He paused before the door to the drawing room, taking a deep breath to calm his nerves and squaring his shoulders before nodding to the footman to announce him.

*****

Georgiana looked up expectantly as the door opened, fully prepared to greet her cousin or some other family member, but was shocked into silence at the footman's announcement. She sent a sideways glare at her sister for not preparing her ahead of time, but Elizabeth only looked on serenely, dropping a subtle wink in Georgiana's direction as she rose to greet their guest.

Georgiana quickly collected herself and welcomed Thaddeus with a warm smile. "Mr. Crosby, it is so good to see you again. I do hope you passed a pleasant winter with your family."

Thaddeus bowed, meeting her eyes over her hand. "It's a pleasure to see you, also, Miss Darcy."

She blushed as he held on to her hand a little longer than propriety dictated. He reluctantly released her hand with a glance toward Darcy, who was doing his best to ignore the interchange between them. Elizabeth looked on openly, a smile on her face.

They shared a shy smile before Elizabeth stepped up and took the lead. "Shall we go in to dinner?"

Elizabeth took her husband's arm and the couple disappeared through the door, leaving Thaddeus to offer his arm to Georgiana. She took it gladly, eagerly striking up a conversation, "Did you get to go ice-skating this winter, Mr. Crosby? It is one of my favorite activities of the season."

He responded enthusiastically, and they made their way to the dining room deep in conversation, picking up as if they had never left off. The evening continued in like vain, with amicable conversation and an almost familial atmosphere. There was a lot of laughter around the dinner table that night as Elizabeth, Georgiana, and Thaddeus joked and teased.

Darcy sat back and watched, imagining many more evenings just like this one. It was a bittersweet moment, realizing that his little sister had grown up and was well on the way to having a family of her own. Her brilliant smile and the way her eyes lit up as she watched Thaddeus left Darcy with an ache in his chest. He was losing her and he knew it. She would never look at him with the same adoration that she bestowed on the man in front of her. She would no longer need him to care for her and provide for her.

It was a sad day for Darcy, realizing he was not the most important man in his sister's life anymore. His wife had been trying to prepare him for that reality for quite some time, but it was only now sinking in.

He remembered fondly the little girl she used to be; hiding behind him when introduced to their formidable aunt, looking up at him with childish awe and adoration in her eyes when he brought her home a gift, finding her concealed in the sideboard cabinets trying to escape her governess.

The confident, sophisticated lady before him no longer resembled the child she used to be. He was proud of the woman she had become.

He turned his thoughts back to the conversation at hand, making an effort to learn more about the man that in all likelihood would soon become part of his family.

Dinner concluded companionably, and Elizabeth and Georgiana repaired to the drawing room, leaving the men to their port. Darcy took advantage of having Thaddeus' full attention to ask, "Have you found a property to invest in? I remember you were hoping to purchase an estate last summer."

"There is one I'm very interested in. There is an estate in the north that is being sold for a very reasonable price…" Thaddeus proceeded to go into further detail, and Darcy couldn't hide his smile. His sister would be very well taken care of indeed.

Elizabeth was surprised by the length of time it took the gentlemen to join them. She had expected them to follow them almost immediately, leaving time for only a cursory separation. When they finally did appear, she was shocked to see Darcy smiling and relaxed. He looked inordinately pleased with himself. She lifted one eyebrow dryly as he met her eyes, but her husband only grinned mischievously.

Thaddeus joined Georgiana on the settee, greeting her with a warm smile. Darcy settled in an arm chair beside the one that his wife was occupying.

"Who came to visit this morning?" Thaddeus asked, hoping to prompt a conversation. "Darcy mentioned earlier that you had been expecting callers."

"Lady Matlock, my aunt, stopped by for a short time," Georgiana responded. "I haven't seen her since last spring, so it was delightful to hear about my cousin, Colonel Fitzwilliam, and his family. The Colonel doesn't visit us at Pemberley as often since he's retired to the countryside with his wife and child. His wife, who is my cousin Anne, doesn't have very good health and the long journey is very difficult for her."

"But," Elizabeth interjected, "Lady Matlock informed us that the country air has done wonders for Mrs. Fitzwilliam's health. She's become quite the gardener, I hear. Supposedly, she has created a new variety of roses. I do hope we will be able to visit them soon and see the results of her hard work."

The couples continued to chat for awhile until Elizabeth suggested, "Would you play something for us, Georgiana?"

Georgiana acquiesced graciously, and Thaddeus joined her at the pianoforte, ostensibly to turn pages. While the two young lovebirds ogled one another across the instrument, Elizabeth turned to her husband.

"What has you looking so smug?" she asked.

Darcy leaned a little closer, and she sat forward, eager to hear his secret.

"You'll just have to wait and find out," he teased her, knowing she hated to be left out of anything. "But trust me, you will be just as excited as I am when you find out. Shall we have the children sent for?"

Elizabeth glared at her husband's lack of disclosure, but agreed to his proposition. She rose to pull the bell. Soon, Thea and Will joined them, playing quietly on the floor.

Meanwhile, Thaddeus and Georgiana were lost in their own little world.

"I believe I recognize this piece," Thaddeus commented, leaning over to look at the music set before her. "And I see that once again you have no need of my services."

Georgiana smiled coyly. "But the company is still much appreciated."

Thaddeus returned the smile, flushed with pleasure at the compliment. "This piece has become quite a favorite of mine, I must confess. I cannot help but be reminded of my visit to Chetborn when I hear it played. It always brings back such fond memories for me."

Thaddeus looked on with delight as Georgiana's cheeks turned a delightful shade of pink. She avoided his eyes as she admitted, "I, too, find I cannot play this piece without thinking of Chetborn." She raised her eyes to his boldly. "I'm afraid my brother and sister have quite tired of hearing it on cold winter evenings locked away at Pemberley."

"I don't think I could ever tire of hearing it played," Thaddeus declared, gazing into Georgiana's eyes. For long, tense moments they stared at each other, Georgiana's hands stilling on the instrument as they lost track of time and place.

A cough from across the room brought them back to earth. Hurriedly, Georgiana picked up where she had left off, stumbling through a few notes in her haste. Thaddeus caught her eye and they shared a rueful smile.

"Perhaps we should stick to more general topics, Mr. Crosby," Georgiana suggested.

"I don't think I could ever discuss something as paltry as the weather with you, Miss Darcy," Thaddeus replied.

She blushed. "Then let us think of something less paltry to discuss. I was informed this morning that your brother and sister are to hold a ball in a few days time. Are you looking forward to being in attendance?"

"As I believe your invitation was delivered personally this morning by my sister, I can only look forward to it with the greatest enthusiasm," Thaddeus commented. "Are you to have a new gown for the occasion?"

Georgiana laughed. "I haven't had time to visit the dressmaker's as we've yet to be in town a full day. There is no way a new gown could be made in time. But I assure you, having never had the opportunity to attend a ball where you were in attendance, you will not recognize whatever gown I chose to wear."

"Ah, but you do plan to do a little shopping while you are in Town?" Thaddeus asked.

"Yes, my sister and I are hoping to do some shopping tomorrow, in fact. My brother has been very generous and patient with us," she said with a laugh. "I know most men do not understand the desire for new things."

"I must confess that I don't quite understand it myself. I am a simple man and have no desire for the frippery that so many seem to prefer. But I do appreciate your brother's desire to see you dressed in fine things and to see you enjoying yourself. I rather enjoy the result myself," Thaddeus admitted with a wink.

She raised an eyebrow at the masculine conceit, but let it pass with no comment. Thaddeus paused and gathered his courage. Hoping not to appear too over eager, he asked, "May I have the pleasure of securing your hand for the first dance?"

She beamed at him, answering simply, "You may."

Thaddeus let out the breath he had been holding and grinned back at her. Once more they were in danger of becoming lost in each other's eyes, oblivious as they were to the rest of the room.

Darcy finally decided to intervene, his patience with the young couple wearing thin. He called his daughter over to him. "Thea, dear, why don't you go ask your aunt to read a story to you?"

The little girl looked up at him very seriously. "I cannot, Papa."

"Why not?" Darcy asked in surprise and irritation.

"Because, Papa, you always tell me not to interrupt grownups when they're talking," she replied earnestly.

Elizabeth hid her smile behind her hand as Darcy frowned, not sure how to respond.

"We'll make an exception this once," Darcy finally said, exasperated. "Go ask her to read you a story, or something."

Thea finally relented, hesitantly crossing the room to Georgiana's side while throwing a questioning look over her shoulder at her father.

Darcy finally met his wife's dancing eyes. "Don't you dare say anything," he warned.

"Oh, you needn't worry about me," his wife replied, laughter evident in her voice. "You just sent the little tattle-tale over to your sister."

Georgiana was surprised at the tug she felt on her dress sleeve. Looking down, she couldn't help but smile at her niece peering up at her, thumb in mouth. She stopped playing and shifted to give the little girl her attention.

"What is it, Thea?" Georgiana asked. "Is something wrong?"

Thea frowned in an expression identical to her father's. "Papa said to ask you to read me a story. I told him it wasn't nice to interrupt grown-ups when they're talkin' but he said to do it anyways."

Georgiana laughed, seeing through her brother's efforts. "I don't know about a story," she said, "but how about you sit here beside me and we can play a duet?"

The little girl smiled. "Okay." She climbed up on the bench beside Georgiana and stretched her short arms out to reach the keys. Her fingers barely grazed them.

"Are you ready?" Georgiana asked.

Thea's brow furrowed in concentration and she kept her eyes firmly on the keys in front of her as she nodded. Together, they picked out a simple nursery song, with very few errors.

Thaddeus watched them play, his heart in his throat. In few years time, he could see a scene very much like this one playing out in his own drawing room, only with his own daughter next to Georgiana on the bench.

He swallowed hard as the song drew to a close, tamping down the emotions that were threatening to overwhelm him. "Very well played, Miss Darcy," he complimented Thea.

She glanced up at him. "I didn't play all the notes right."

Georgiana hastened to reassure her. "That's okay. That is why we practice- so we can get better and play all the notes correctly. You played that piece very well considering that you've only practiced it a few times with me."

"I enjoyed hearing you play very much." Thaddeus added, "Do you know another song you could play for me?"

Thea's chest puffed out with pride. "I know one I can play all by myself." Georgiana sat back and Thea leaned forward in concentration once more.

Elizabeth watched her daughter play contentedly, warm with motherly pride. Her son had fallen asleep on his father's lap, unused to such late hours. She met her husband's eyes and couldn't resist teasing him, "I think your plan backfired, dear."

"I know," he said long-sufferingly, "but at least I get to watch my beautiful daughter enjoy herself at the piano. She takes after you, you know."

Elizabeth laughed. "I know you claim my musical ability surpasses all others, but truly I would be most pleased if she took after Georgiana and not me in this case. Georgiana has the patience to teach her and help her practice. I would be a poor substitute, for I never could be prevailed upon to practice. Mary quite despised of me."

There was glint in her husband's eye as he recalled their early acquaintance and how enamored of her playing he had been then. He remembered fondly bragging to Georgiana of her prowess long before he had believed there was any hope of a courtship between them. He still enjoyed watching her perform, ignoring the few mistakes she invariably made. In his eyes, there was no woman that could compare to his wife.

Elizabeth reached over to pat her husband's hand, her tone softening, "I could perhaps be convinced to play a tune or two, a little later."

Darcy turned his hand over and intertwined their fingers, careless of the company. Gently, he allowed his thumb to caress the back of his wife's hand as he gazed into her eyes. "I'd like that very much, my dear."

Darcy rose from his seat, releasing his wife's hand as Thea's song ended. He picked the little girl up and settled her on his lap, usurping her seat to join his sister at the instrument.

"That was very well done indeed, Thea," Darcy complimented his daughter. "But now, why don't we let your Mama have a chance to showcase her talents?"

Georgiana laughed, good-naturedly rising from the bench at her brother's pleading look. "Yes, Elizabeth, do come entertain us. I know my brother will not be content until you do."

The company took their seats as Elizabeth settled herself at the bench, casting once last wry glance at her husband before she launched into her piece.

"Brother loves to listen to my sister at the pianoforte," Georgiana explained to Thaddeus in a low voice. "It dates back to their courtship. Every now and then she allows herself to be coerced into performing among family just to please him."

Thaddeus glanced over at Darcy, who was paying rapt attention to his wife, although he was restrained from joining her at the instrument by the child asleep on his lap.

A few discordant notes rent the air, and Georgiana stifled her instinctive flinch. Thaddeus smiled as he noticed her fingers twitching, longing to correct the missed notes. Darcy's smile only widened at Elizabeth's mistake; he only had eyes for his wife.

It was evident by the time that Elizabeth effortlessly slipped into her second piece that the evening was drawing to a close, no matter how the young lovers may have dreaded it. Thea was nodding off in her chair, jerking briefly to consciousness as her head fell forward before her eyes began to droop again.

Thaddeus had intersected a significant glance between Elizabeth and Darcy, and knew that he would have to excuse himself when Elizabeth rose from the instrument. He had no desire to overstay his welcome, especially so early in the game.

As it was, he considered the evening a great success. He had been welcomed into their home and been treated as a member of the family. He knew that the night would be among his most treasured memories for many years to come.

Elizabeth concluded the light folk song she had been playing gracefully and stood to take a slight bow as her audience applauded. Darcy clapped loudly and enthusiastically, the noise waking the sleeping boy on his lap. Will immediately sat up and began wailing, unhappy to be woken from his peaceful slumber. Elizabeth rushed to take her baby, cuddling and shushing him as Darcy stood to ring for the nurse.

Thaddeus turned to Georgiana. "I think that is my cue to take my leave."

He rose and addressed Mr. and Mrs. Darcy, "I want to thank you for a wonderful evening. I have never enjoyed myself quite so much as I have tonight. I hope I will be able to return the favor in the not so distant future." He turned to address Georgiana again, "May I ask, Miss Darcy, if you would favor me with your company for a turn about the park tomorrow morning?"

Her cheeks took on a rosy tinge as she murmured, "I should like that very much, indeed."

His goal accomplished, he bowed and took his leave of the company.

Soon after, the nurse arrived to collect the children and take them off to bed. Georgiana quickly excused herself afterwards, needing some privacy to process the day's events.

She submitted meekly to her maid's efforts, allowing her to help her out of her evening gown and into her nightdress, but balked when the young woman made to take down her hair.

"You can leave that, Alice. I have no further need of you." The young woman's startled eyes flew to meet Georgiana's in the looking glass, unused to such brusqueness from her mistress. Georgiana softened her tone, "I'd like some time to myself now, if you don't mind, Alice. It has been a rather exciting day."

Alice's eyes lightened with a knowingly look and she flashed a cheeky pair of dimples as she curtsied. "Yes, ma'am."

Georgiana couldn't bring herself to be annoyed with the young woman as she closed the door behind her. It was obvious that all the servants knew that something was going on between Thaddeus and her. She had caught whispers of it through the halls as she had returned to her room. It was equally obvious that the servants had nothing but their best wishes for her future happiness.

She returned to gazing at herself in the mirror, admiring her maid's handiwork for a last few moments before reaching up to take out the first pin. Soon, her hair spilled down around her shoulders, shimmering like gold in the candlelight.

She picked up her brush and began to stroke her hair, watching the fine, silken strands as they fell back into place and wishing idly for Elizabeth's luxurious brunette curls. Sighing, she resigned herself to being content with her own strands, and quickly plaited her flaxen locks into a simple braid.

Even though she was technically ready for bed, her mind was still racing, her thoughts in turmoil. She settled herself on her stomach across the bed and placed her chin in her hands, the girlish pose bringing a slight smile to her lips. She idly picked at a few loose threads on the bed spread and allowed herself to replay the night's activities in her mind, her smile growing.

*****

Darcy and Elizabeth retired to their room, having seen their children tucked into bed without the usual complaints and requests for bedtime stories. The couple held their tongues until the staff had cleared the room, leaving them to each other.

"Well, I think tonight went rather well, don't you?" Elizabeth asked, seating herself on the edge of the bed.

Darcy slid under the covers on his side of the bed, taking a moment to formulate his response. Finally, he responded, tongue in cheek, "I suppose so, if you consider being completely ignored by your guest for half the night to be a good thing."

Elizabeth giggled. "I know very well that you didn't really mind. Georgiana certainly seemed to enjoy herself, and that is all you really care about, or you never would have invited him for dinner." She settled herself beside her husband and smiled coyly. "Now, what was it that had you so full of yourself earlier?"

Darcy grinned broadly, and proceeded to fill her in, much to her delight.

Chapter 8

Georgiana was ready, dressed, and waiting eagerly in the drawing room a good twenty minutes before Thaddeus could be expected the next morning. Elizabeth joined her in the drawing room, ready to act as chaperone if necessary. She picked up her embroidery, watching with a small smile as Georgiana paced the confines of the room, looking remarkably like her brother.

She paused by the window with a huff to quickly scan the road below before setting off across the room again.

Elizabeth glanced up from her embroidery and said with the hint of a smile in her voice, "You're going to wear a path in the carpets if you keep that up, dear."

Georgiana shot her an exasperated look and flopped down in an armchair across from Elizabeth. "I don't know how you can be so calm," she complained. "I almost feel that I shall have to start complaining of my "poor nerves" in order to gain some sympathy."

Elizabeth laughed, even though she knew Georgiana would not appreciate her lively humor at the moment. "Oh my, how very much like my mother you sound."

Georgiana smiled grudgingly, allowing some of the tension to release from her shoulders.

"I'm sorry, dearest," she apologized. "That was very poor form of me to abuse your mother in such a way. Do say you'll forgive me?"

Elizabeth smiled reassuringly. "You know I will, Georgiana. I understand that you're a little nervous. But now that the first meeting is over, surely any further meetings can only be looked upon with pleasure."

"Yes," Georgiana agreed. "Truly, I am looking forward to walking out with Mr. Crosby." She rose from her chair and reclaimed her position by the window. "I do hope he arrives soon."

Elizabeth managed to suppress her chuckle this time. She diligently returned to her embroidery, noting ruefully that her stitches had wandered far off the pattern as she had talked. She began to pick out the work of the last ten minutes, wishing vainly for her sister Kitty's talent for needlework.

They remained thus for some time, Elizabeth bent over her hoop, and Georgiana peering anxiously out the window, until Georgiana suddenly straightened and called excitedly, "He's here! He's finally here! Oh, I do hope he didn't see me at the window!"

She hurried to seat herself, adjusting her skirts nervously and putting a hand up to check that none of her hair was out of place. She looked the very picture of ladylike decorum when the footman announced Thaddeus.

The ladies rose gracefully to meet him, and a few scant minutes later, Elizabeth was watching from an upstairs window as the couple emerged on the street. They were already deep in conversation, ignorant of anything going on around them and the maid following a discreet distance behind them. Elizabeth felt a deep sense of satisfaction, watching Georgiana conversing so easily with Thaddeus. *They will do well together,* she thought to herself. Georgiana had finally found someone she could be comfortable with.

*****

Georgiana returned a while later, glowing. Elizabeth had asked the servants to inform her of her sister's arrival, so she was still divesting herself of her outer garments when Elizabeth appeared in the entryway.

"How was your turn about the park?" Elizabeth asked.

Georgiana beamed at her, stars in her eyes. "We had the most wonderful time! We went down to the pond and saw the swans. It was so lovely!"

"I'm glad you enjoyed yourself," Elizabeth replied, before bringing up her real concern. "Are you still up for some shopping yet today?"

"What?" Georgiana asked. "Oh, I had completely forgotten! I can be ready to leave in a quarter hour if you like."

"That sounds good," Elizabeth commented. "I'll order the carriage and then I just have to speak with Mrs. Cole briefly before we can go."

*****

Soon thereafter, the ladies found themselves comfortably ensconced at their dressmakers, enjoying some tea and scones while they poured through the latest fashion plates.

"Oooo," Elizabeth cooed. "This one is gorgeous! That style would look lovely on your tall frame, Georgiana." She tipped the page so Georgiana could see it.

"That *is* lovely," Georgiana agreed. "Have you found anything you fancy for yourself? I know Brother would want you to choose something you like as well."

"Well, I had thought about this dress for myself." She showed Georgiana the fashion plate she was looking at. "But I'm not sure if I can pull it off as I'm so petite. What do you think?"

Georgiana perused the design for a few moments in silence before responding. "I think as long as you make some adjustments here, here, and here," she pointed to the offending areas, "then it will be very flattering on your figure."

Elizabeth thanked Georgiana for her insight, and went on to pick out two more patterns before moving on to fabrics. Georgiana took her time, picking out two new ball gowns, several new morning gowns, and a riding habit. Soon though, she too was knee deep in fabric swatches, ribbons, and gloves.

The women emerged much later, giddy over their selections. They handed over a few bags with some small trinkets to the waiting servant, but most of their purchases would be brought to the town house in a few days time for their first fitting.

Darcy heard their girlish laughter from his study as they lingered in the entryway removing their outerwear. He couldn't help but smile. It was well worth the great deal of money they had spent to know they were enjoying themselves so well. He heard Elizabeth ask Mrs. Cole where he was, and returned to perusing the paperwork in front of him, trying to appear busy.

She knocked lightly on the door and he looked up with a smile to welcome her in.

"Did you have a good time, dearest?" he asked as she came around the desk to seat herself on his lap.

"The best," she responded, punctuating her words with a kiss.

He chuckled. "You must have spent a great deal to warrant such a display of affection. Have you come to ask my forgiveness? Or to inform me we shall have to make our home in a poorhouse?"

She laughed. "I doubt very much I could ever spend all the money you have squirreled away. And I know very well that you would not want me to be at a disadvantage among the other ladies of the ton. Nor would you wish for your sister to have a harder time in company than she already does." She batted her eyes flirtatiously. "Besides, I think you will rather approve of some of the gowns I chose."

"You know me quite well," Darcy acknowledged, returning her kiss. They remained thus, quite agreeably engaged for a few minutes.

Finally, they broke apart and she slid off his lap with a sigh. "I suppose I ought to go speak with Mrs. Cole about dinner."

He watched appreciatively as she walked out the room, turning back to his work with a sigh as she closed the door behind her. How could he be expected to get any work done after such a pleasant distraction?

*****

The night of the Crosby's ball rolled around before they knew it. Georgiana waited nervously in the parlor for her brother and sister to appear. In an effort to quell her incessant pacing, she paused in front of the mirror to inspect herself once more.

The recent change in fashion towards more saturated colors had stood her in good stead. Her gown was deep emerald, with gold embroidery along the bodice and hem line. Her eyes had morphed to match the dress, shining like jewels in the candlelight.

The dress was fitted under her bust, the skirt flaring out conically from under the bodice. She found the trend toward fuller, more modest skirts to be somewhat of a relief after the clinging, diaphanous fabrics of the past few years. The lace edging along the neckline helped preserve her modesty as well, even though she knew there would be many that had no such qualms.

She knew that many of the ladies present at the ball would be sporting several flounces at the hemline, but she preferred a simpler style, so had opted to do with only one. She only hoped that the divergence from the latest trend would not bring too much ridicule from her contemporaries.

She had kept her jewelry simple as well, wearing only a thin gold necklace dotted with pearls rather than her more ostentatious family pieces. Her requisite white gloves had bunched around her elbows.

Her gaze traveled upward to inspect her hair. Her fine blond locks had been prettily arranged in the latest fashion, parted down the middle and curled into tight ringlets over her ears. The rest of her hair had been braided and wound into a bun at the back of her head, ribbons intertwined through the plaits.

She was satisfied with her appearance. Her maid had been very pleased with the results of her handiwork, and Georgiana could find no fault with it herself. Still, she was anxious. Even though she was clothed in the latest styles, Miranda Rycroft always found something about her to snicker about.

She sighed and turned away from the mirror, feeling somewhat dejected. She had tried so hard to fit in, to keep herself under firm regulation, but in the end it did not matter. Miranda Rycroft and her gaggle of friends were always there to taunt her.

An evening that had begun with keen anticipation was suddenly shadowed by her unseen nemesis. Georgiana heard the first whispers of voices in the hall, signaling the arrival of her brother and sister.

No matter, she thought to herself, *You are a Darcy, and Darcys do not back down. Besides, Thaddeus will be there, and he will appreciate your efforts.*

She squared her shoulders and lifted her chin determinedly. *It will be a wonderful evening,* she thought resolutely, *because regardless of what Miranda might say, I am determined to enjoy myself!*

Elizabeth and Darcy appeared in the doorway. "Are you ready to leave?"

*****

Georgiana gazed around the well-lit entryway of the Crosby's townhouse. The flickering candles reflected in the marble floors and crystal chandeliers. The room echoed with greetings, voices carrying in the cavernous space of the two story entry. The heady scent of the copious floral arrangements mixed with the smell of the numerous perfumed bodies crowding the space, creating an almost overwhelming aroma.

Feeling a little sick to her stomach, Georgiana moved to join the receiving line with her brother and Elizabeth, allowing more people to flood in through the doors behind her. The line seemed infinitely long to Georgiana, who was already becoming uncomfortable in the crush of people. Elizabeth was laughing gaily with the woman in front of her, unaffected by the crowd. Darcy had pasted a smile on his face that was quickly disappearing to be replaced with his stony mask.

Finally, they reached the head of the line, ready to greet their hosts for the evening and move on. All of Georgiana's discomfort fled momentarily as she met Thaddeus' eyes. He stepped forward with a smile to greet her, bowing over her hand.

"I do hope, Miss Darcy, you remembered your first set is promised to me?" Thaddeus asked, not wanting to leave the matter to chance.

Georgiana blushed and murmured that she had, indeed, remembered and graced him with an answering smile before the line moved forward and she was forced to part ways with him.

"Miss Darcy, how delightful it is to see you!" Caroline cooed, as they made their bows. "I'm so glad you were able to make it to our modest little party."

Georgiana noticed her brother raise one sardonic eyebrow at the greeting, but she chose to respond politely as Elizabeth shot her husband a reproving glance.

"It is a delight to see you as well, Mrs. Crosby, Mr. Crosby," she murmured. "Everything looks lovely."

There was no time for further discussion as more guests demanded Alfred and Caroline's attention. Relieved to have made it through the first hurdle, Georgiana followed her brother and sister into the ballroom.

People were milling about everywhere, waiting for the dancing to start. A grand chandelier presided over the space, and an elaborate floral pattern had been chalked on the center of the dance floor to protect the dancers from the slipping on the waxed floor.

Georgiana could see that refreshments had been set up in the next room over; the double doors invited any and all to partake of the bounty laid out there. Unfortunately, Georgiana could tell too many had already overindulged in the beverages laid out. She wrinkled her nose at the stench of alcohol coming off an older man as he stumbled by her.

She transferred her gaze from the refreshment table to sweep the room, carefully taking in every detail. Footmen and servants were stationed at regular intervals, ready to help any guest that needed their services. Georgiana recognized some new faces among the familiar ones of the Crosby's staff. They must have hired some additional help for the occasion.

The Crosby's had certainly spared no expense.

Georgiana looked around her for a familiar face, but she spent most of her time in the country and Caroline's sphere of friends was quite different than hers. The genial Bingleys would have been included in the invitations, but they would not be in attendance this close to Jane's confinement. She knew they were safely ensconced at Chetborn, awaiting their new arrival anxiously.

She sighed and allowed her brother to escort her to a seat along the walls. She had no desire to draw attention to herself by lingering in the doorway.

Darcy found them seats near a group of young matrons that Elizabeth and Georgiana knew from a few seasons previously. The women turned down his offer of refreshments, leaving Darcy free to find one of his old university friends to talk to. Georgiana smiled as he quickly relegated himself to a corner of the ballroom, deep in conversation, drink in hand. It was good to see her brother actually enjoying himself for the moment.

Georgiana sat at the edge of the group, listening to the conversation going on around her, only occasionally pitching in with an opinion or comment. She anxiously awaited the start of the dancing and the arrival of Thaddeus to claim her first set.

Elizabeth, on the other hand, with her easy manners and friendly nature, was already enjoying herself, making the young women around them laugh lightly with her charming wit. She was at her best in the ballroom, gregarious and pleasant. Georgiana watched her with a twinge of jealousy for her ease in company, especially among those she did not know well.

The musicians began to tune their instruments, signaling the start of the dancing. The room began to stir restlessly, awaiting the arrival of the host and hostess to begin the dancing. Finally, the Crosby's took to the floor, and Thaddeus appeared out of the crowd to claim Georgiana's hand.

She greeted him with a brilliant smile. The pleasure in her eyes at the sight of him made him pause momentarily in his steps, before an answering smile lit up his face. He took the last few steps to reach her side.

She eagerly placed her gloved hand in his outstretched one, allowing him to pull her to her feet. They took their places in the set.

"You look lovely tonight, Miss Darcy. That gown compliments your eyes beautifully," Thaddeus told Georgiana.

She lowered her eyes shyly and demurred, "You are too kind, Mr. Crosby. If you are not careful, your flattery will go to my head and I shall become impossible to deal with." Inwardly, she was pleased with his compliments. It was nice to know her efforts with her appearance were appreciated.

Thaddeus laughed. "I doubt very much that someone with your modesty and humility would allow a simple compliment to go to their head in such a way. But I shall change the topic to one you find less objectionable. Come; tell me how you have been spending your time these last few days."

She latched on to the topic. "Not in a way that would you interest you, I fear. My sister and I have been spending most of our time shopping and stocking up on handkerchiefs, slippers, and other such necessities."

"Have you ordered some new gowns as well?" Thaddeus asked.

"Of course," Georgiana assured him. "My brother insisted that we commission several new gowns for ourselves. We had our first fittings at the townhouse a few days ago." She developed a teasing glint in her eye. "It wouldn't do to embarrass ourselves in society by wearing last year's fashions."

"No, that would be disastrous," Thaddeus deadpanned. "You would never live it down." He sighed. "I'm sure that your week was spent much more pleasantly than mine. I spent most of my time trying to avoid my sister and the myriad of errands she wanted me to run in preparation for the ball tonight. When she wasn't trying to recruit me for something or another, she was on the rampage, barking out orders. I just tried to stay out of the way."

"I can imagine it wasn't a very agreeable way to spend the week," Georgiana said sympathetically. But she felt compelled to point out, "At least you weren't one of the servants who had to answer her every beck and call. You could escape."

"Yes, and I did. Were you aware that there is a very pleasant little park right around the corner from here?" Thaddeus asked. "I discovered it this week during my wanderings."

"I can't say I've been there, as my brother prefers I stay closer to home," Georgiana said, amused. "But I was aware of its existence. My maid, Alice, often journeys there on her time off to visit her beau, who works for one of the families on this street. It is not terribly far of a walk from our townhouse."

"Perhaps your brother will allow you to venture to the park under my escort and we can explore it together," Thaddeus suggested. "Do you think he would approve that plan?"

"He might be a bit hesitant," Georgiana replied with a light laugh. "But I could appeal to my sister and she might be able to persuade him. She is always encouraging him to allow me more independence and she holds more sway over him than I do."

"Wives have a tendency to do so," Thaddeus said, "and Mrs. Darcy is not a woman to take things sitting down. I imagine she could be quite persuasive."

"She can be," Georgiana agreed. "In the five years they've been married, I've seen a remarkable change in my brother. He is ever so much more relaxed and open to new ideas than he used to be. He was always the best of brothers, but Elizabeth brings out the very best in him. She has been a good influence on the both of us."

Thaddeus looked at her, a soft gleam in his eye. "I certainly appreciate the result of her influence."

Georgiana blushed and they were silent as the steps of the dance separated them. The remainder of the set was spent in much the same way, with amicable conversation and light footwork on both parts. Finally though, their time together was up, and Thaddeus escorted her back to her seat. Bowing over her hand, he asked, "I do hope you will reserve the supper dance for me, as well?"

She assured him she would, as her card was not already filled and she had particularly reserved that set for him, hoping he would ask her. Reluctantly they parted ways, each to a different partner. For the first time, Georgiana found herself chaffing under the rules of propriety, allowing them only two sets together. How she wished they could dance the night away, without the requisite separation!

Instead, she could only watch from afar as he led another young lady to the dance floor. She was called back to her senses by the arrival of her own partner. She greeted the young man, an acquaintance from past seasons, with a stiff smile and allowed herself to be led on to the dance floor.

A few sets later, Georgiana was resting, waiting for her partner to return with refreshments. She looked around the large ballroom aimlessly, watching the people that had gathered. There was a group of matrons seated near the refreshments, fanning themselves and gossiping over their drinks. A cluster of men were gathered in a corner, discussing politics and business. A few young ladies sat along the edges of the dance floor, resting or pining for partners of their own.

A flash of obnoxious tangerine caught Georgiana's eye, and her attention was immediately arrested by the sight of her nemesis, Miranda Rycroft, standing next to Caroline Crosby.

She sized the young woman up, begrudgingly noting that she looked exceptionally beautiful. Her gown was a lovely aquamarine, designed to exactly match the blue eyes she was so well-known for. Her shimmering chestnut locks were styled similarly to Georgiana's own, but with strands of pearls and jewels woven through the more elaborate design. Her bodice was cut a little too low for Georgiana's modest tastes, but it was still well within the bounds of propriety. She wore sapphires around her white throat and wrists, flaunting her family's wealth. Her dainty features were schooled into a pleasant smile, but Georgiana well knew the venom that she could spew.

Caroline was motioning for someone to join them, and Georgiana's gaze was drawn to the recipient of that gesture by a slight motion in her peripheral vision.

It was Thaddeus! Her Thaddeus! She watched in horror as Caroline introduced the two, and then as Thaddeus and Miranda made their way on to the dance floor. They monopolized her attention as she agonized over every light touch and turn they made around the dance floor.

She noted every lilting laugh that came from Miranda and every pleasant smile that Thaddeus afforded his partner. Her heart sank. The couple looked like they were having a marvelous time together. She knew Miranda would not give up easily if she set her sights on Thaddeus as the object of her affections.

Georgiana's doubts threatened to overwhelm her. Suddenly, she felt like an ugly duckling compared to Miranda's beautiful swan. Her clothes were too plain, her hair wasn't as shiny and full, her manners were not as open and vivacious. What did she have to offer that Miranda didn't? She was even an accomplished pianist, known for her ease of performance. Georgiana had never had the confidence to perform for large crowds.

She watched them with a growing sense of unease until her own partner returned, bearing refreshments.

"I apologize for leaving you alone for so long," the young man said, handing her a glass. "There was a jolly long line."

Georgiana sipped her ratafia and allowed him to chatter on, only responding with a nod or an indistinguishable murmur whenever it was incumbent upon her to say something. Outwardly she was cool and collected, her Darcy mask firmly in place, but inwardly she was churning with anxiety. How could she compete with Miranda?

Eventually, her more rational self began to reassert itself. She had a history with Thaddeus that Miranda did not. They had spent several weeks together at Chetborn, and their reunion earlier that week had left her hopeful for her future. She had every reason to believe that things would be fine. With those thoughts in mind, she was able to relax a little and tune back into her partner, who thankfully had not seemed to notice her distraction.

The set finally ended, and Georgiana was relieved to see her young man go, only to be surprised to find Thaddeus escorting Miranda to a seat near her. Her heart sunk a little, for that meant that Miranda had noticed her presence and she had no way of knowing what the other young woman intended by seeking her out.

Feeling apprehensive, Georgiana schooled her features into a polite smile, keeping herself under tight regulation. Now was not the time to lose her rigid control and allow Miranda an opportunity to exploit her weaknesses.

"Miss Darcy," Thaddeus said with a smile. "I believe you are familiar with Miss Rycroft. She has been telling me how particularly she wanted to renew your acquaintance."

"How kind," Georgiana murmured, inwardly knowing differently.

"I shall leave you two ladies here to catch up," Thaddeus said. "I'm sure you have much to speak about and I would only be a hindrance." He bowed and left them, with only a single backwards glance at Georgiana that she was too blind to notice.

"Miss Darcy, what a pleasure to see you finally in Town again," Miranda purred, a false smile on her face. "I was afraid you would miss all the festivities this year coming so late in the season."

Georgiana smiled stiffly, wondering what game was afoot. "Yes, well, we had to wait until the roads were sound enough to travel. It is quite a journey from Pemberley."

She didn't have long to wait to find out.

"That's too bad," Miranda said with a glimmer in her eye. "You've missed so much already. Why, just last week Mr. Crosby and I attended the Wilkinson's musical soiree. La, what a laugh that was! We had the most amusing conversation. Then, just a few days later, when he came to call, we went driving and we heard the most interesting bit of gossip. You will never guess who is down in the duns now!" She paused and abruptly changed topics, giving Georgiana a significant look. "Anyway, with such a start to the season I think it may well be my last on the marriage mart. I have every reason to expect to share some good news very soon."

Georgiana sat rigid in her seat, a smile painted on her face, for a long moment, trying to come up with some sort of reply. Finally, she replied coolly, "You will understand if I withhold my congratulations until the happy event takes place. I do wish you all the best. Now, if you will excuse me, Miss Rycroft, I really must attend to my sister."

She rose and began to make her way along the outer edge of the courtyard to the hall beyond, taking no note of the triumphant look on Miranda Rycroft's face. She went blindly, not paying attention to where she was going or who was around her; she only looked for the quiet and solitude she desired.

She found them eventually, in the empty library. There was a dying fire in the grate, enough to provide some light but nothing more. There would have been no reason to keep the room heated on a night when the entire household would be concentrated in the public rooms of the house.

She shivered a little at the draft in the room and went to find a seat by fire. She pulled a small footstool near the hearth, feeling like a little girl again, sitting at her brother's feet. Her mind whirred with thoughts and emotions, not knowing what to think and feel. She took several deep, cleansing breaths, trying to calm her thoughts so she could make sense of all that was racing through her mind.

"Okay," Georgiana told herself. "There is no reason to jump to conclusions. I know Miranda to be malicious and jealous. She could just be trying to cause problems and create an opportunity for herself after seeing Thaddeus and I together earlier. But I have no way of knowing if she is telling the truth about the time they spent together. And it is obvious that Caroline is encouraging her in her pursuit of Mr. Crosby. Oh, what to think!"

She groaned and lowered her head into her hands. She replayed their conversations in her mind, looking for hidden meanings and objectives. Could she have missed some sign that there was nothing really between them? She sat thus for some time, until finally she knew she would have to return to the ballroom, or someone would miss her presence and come searching for her.

She settled her mask in place, and adopted a distant, cool air. Prepared to face the crowds yet again, she ventured forth from the library once more. She wove her way through the throngs to reach her sister's side.

Perhaps she would have been able to ignore Miranda's comments as the barbs they were if she had not happened to pass behind two portly matrons at that moment.

"Who is that handsome young man that seems to have been monopolizing Miranda Rycroft's attention these past few weeks?"

Georgiana could not help but pause at hearing the question. She was torn between her desire to know the answer, and the possibility of getting caught listening to someone else's conversation.

"Why, that is Mr. Thaddeus Crosby, of course. He is the younger brother of Mr. Alfred Crosby. I hear he has five thousand a year and is looking for a property to buy," the lady answered her friend. "He is expected to propose any day. Of course, Mrs. Crosby favors the match as Miss Rycroft is one of her particular friends. But if you ask me, I think he's more interested in courting her ten thousand pound dowry than her."

Georgiana started as the older women giggled behind their fans and blushed as she realized the impropriety of what she was doing. She hurried away to find Elizabeth, her mind whirring with this new information. She had not expected to have Miranda's words confirmed so credibly. Surely, if it was so well known, if it had been observed by so many to be thus, it must be true! How else could what she had just overheard be explained?

She joined her sister and Elizabeth leaned over to whisper to her from behind her fan, "Are you quite all right dear? You seemed to have wandered off."

"I'm fine," Georgiana reassured her, "I just needed some air. It is terribly stuffy in here."

Elizabeth, unknowing of all that had transpired, saw no further reason to question her, and so replied with a laugh, pointing in Darcy's direction, "Yes, I believe your brother is in need of some air himself. But as the supper dance is coming up next, he should be able to get the respite he needs soon."

Georgiana was taken aback by the mention of the supper dance. Had that much time passed already? Was she to face Mr. Crosby so soon?

It seemed she was, for here he came as the last set broke apart. She stiffened her spine and forced a smile to her lips. She was a Darcy. She could do this.

"Miss Darcy," Thaddeus said, bowing over her hand. "I do believe this dance belongs to me."

"So it does," she said coolly, allowing him to lead her on to the dance floor. She avoided his eyes as they took their place in the set.

Thaddeus was a little confused by Georgiana's cool demeanor, but he dismissed her behavior as her shy nature asserting itself in the crowded ballroom. He redoubled his efforts to draw her out.

"Have you enjoyed yourself this evening?" he asked.

"I have," Georgiana replied shortly, keeping her eyes downcast.

"It is remarkable how many couples are dancing. Even your brother and sister are on the floor for the supper dance. I believe it's causing quite a stir," Thaddeus remarked.

This brought Georgiana's head up briefly as she glanced at where her brother and sister were dancing with a smile. "Yes, my brother always dances the supper dance with my sister. I think it makes the matrons jealous to see the affection between them."

Thaddeus grinned and peeked over at the group of older women in the corner, who were all watching the other couple intently, envy written on their faces.

It was quite a show of favor on Darcy's part to dance with his wife at a social gathering, especially as his reticence towards dancing was well known among the members of the Ton. Since his marriage, he had deemed himself no longer obligated to dance with the many maidens that longed for a partner. But he still favored his lively wife with the supper set because as he knew, she not only dearly loved to laugh, she also dearly loved to dance. He could not deny her that.

The Darcys only had eyes for each other, unaware of the commotion they were making among the members of the Ton. Thaddeus noted Georgiana's softened countenance with pleasure as she turned back to him. Having succeeded in his efforts, he turned his attention to enjoying the dance.

Georgiana danced very well, considering her brother's aversion to the activity. Much of that was due to Elizabeth's influence in the household and her insistence that Georgiana be prepared for the rigors of a season in Town. Thaddeus reflected pleasurably on her lightness of foot and elegance of carriage, unaware of the control that kept her emotions just as rigidly in check.

They completed the set in silence and Georgiana was relieved when he led her into the dining room, finding her a seat at a small table to one side of the room. She briefly enjoyed a small respite from her conflicting emotions as he went to fix their plates. She set aside her own difficulties, choosing instead to focus on watching the people around her as she waited.

Distracted thus, she remained ignorant of the danger approaching until a grating voice cut in on her ruminations.

"Why, how fortunate that these seats aren't already taken," Miranda purred, seating herself across the table. "For I did *so* want to speak to you, Georgiana dear."

Georgiana managed a tight smile in response to the other woman's over-familiarity, but had no opportunity to speak as Miranda went on without pause.

"Since our families are to be *so* closely connected very shortly I thought it incumbent on me to develop our acquaintance further. I do hope that we shall become good friends." Miranda punctuated her words with a cat-like smile, aware that she was toying with her mouse.

The arrival of their respective partners put an end to Miranda's effusions as she bestowed a beaming smile upon Thaddeus.

"Why, Mr. Crosby!" she exclaimed. "What a pleasure to find that you are sharing a table with us! I was just telling Georgiana how I positively despise being seated beside those I have little acquaintance with."

Thaddeus glanced at Georgiana, taken aback by Miranda's simultaneous onslaught on him and disregard for her partner. But her head was down and her gaze focused on the food in front of her, even as she poked and prodded without tasting any of it.

Left on his own, he could only respond politely, "Indeed, I am sure that we will enjoy the pleasure of your company as well."

Fortunately for Miranda, her partner was a rather taciturn fellow, who had no real interest in pursuing a conversation while there was good food to be eaten and good wine to be drunk. She was thus free to continue in like manner without fear of an interruption from that party.

She laughed lightly. "You are too kind Mr. Crosby. Tell me, have you heard any more news about Lord -, since we were driving in the park? I do so love to hear the latest gossip."

Thaddeus shifted uncomfortably in his seat at the distasteful topic. "No, I fear I have heard no more about the poor fellow. I do hope he is able to overcome this latest setback." He felt keenly the inappropriateness of the spread of the gossip and wished intently that Miranda would change the subject.

Georgiana's hand froze momentarily in pushing her food around her plate. In her shock, she did not distinguish Thaddeus' distaste for the subject, only the confirmation that he had indeed been driving with Miranda.

Miranda noted the pause triumphantly, and plowed on in her quest. "I confess I was quite shocked that Lady – dared to show her face at your brother and sister's card party the other evening with all the rumors flying about."

Georgiana resumed pushing her food around with unusual vigor. Thaddeus' attention was drawn by the sudden movement and he frowned as he noticed how little she had actually eaten.

"Miss Darcy, I can't help but notice that your food does not seem to your liking. Would you prefer I bring you something else from the buffet?" Thaddeus asked, his brow creased with concern.

Georgiana looked up, startled at the sudden attention, before hurrying to reassure him, "No, no, Mr. Crosby. This is fine. Thank you." She stuffed a bite in her mouth to prove her claims.

He did not look reassured, but Miranda claimed his attention before he could press the issue. Georgiana returned to prodding her food in relief.

"Yes, well, as I was saying," Miranda went on, annoyed by the interruption, "at the card party the other night…"

And so it continued throughout supper. Miranda talked effusively of every event that she and Thaddeus had ever been in attendance at; Thaddeus tried to alternate between responding politely to Miranda and trying to draw his own partner out; and Georgiana stubbornly refused to look up from rearranging her peas. Meanwhile, Miranda's partner gleefully partook of his meal, unabashedly ignoring his table mates.

Thaddeus could not help but feel that somehow supper had turned into quite a fiasco, but he did not fully realize the extent of the damage until he delivered Georgiana to her sister afterwards, per her request.

He retreated to join a cluster of young men, where he could look like he was listening to their conversation while observing his beloved from afar.

Georgiana's back was to him, but he watched with mounting alarm as Elizabeth's face betrayed a growing concern while Georgiana spoke with her. She ushered the younger woman out of the room, only pausing in the doorway to catch her husband's eye. Thaddeus saw the exchange between husband and wife, the unspoken words that flew between them across the floor. He saw the alarm on Darcy's face and the quickness with which he excused himself from his conversation and followed them out.

Thaddeus tamped down his own urge to rush after them and find out what had happened. As a member of the family party, he could not simply go missing from the ball. It would cause gossip. He forced himself to put on a smile and maintain some vestige of normalcy, all the while keeping one eye on the door, awaiting their return.

But they did not return.

The night dragged on until finally, just as the first rays of dawn were breaking over the horizon, they saw off the last of the carriages.

Thaddeus could contain himself no longer. He turned to his sister, who was leaning against her husband, content in the knowledge of the success of her ball.

"What happened to the Darcys?" he asked. "I didn't see them after supper at all."

Caroline shrugged nonchalantly. "Georgiana had a headache. They went home." She and Alfred turned and went into the house.

Thaddeus remained standing on the front stoop, hardly noticing the chill in the air as he cast his mind back on the night that had just passed.

What had happened to cause Georgiana to plead a headache? Granted, dinner had been a little contrived, but, as he now admitted to himself, her behavior towards him had been markedly changed before that. A sharp gust of wind reminded him that he was still standing outside and he turned to go in, still confused by the evening's events.

*****

Georgiana lay awake as the first rays of sunlight filtered through her curtains. Her tear-stained cheeks attested to the despair she felt and the sleepless night she had passed, even as her unseeing eyes focused on the remnants of the candle that had burned itself out at her bedside.

The truth of Miranda's words had been confirmed by Thaddeus' acknowledgment of the time they had spent together. She had no hope. She would have to bear their eventual engagement with dignity and graciousness. She would harden her heart against

Thaddeus, for she did not think she could bear seeing them together in company otherwise. It was all she could do.

She was blind to all reason on the subject, as love often is. She closed her heart to their time spent together, to the memories they had made and the fond words they had shared. She told herself that she had misunderstood his intentions, that his seeming affections had been those of a friend, not those of a man in love.

She was resolved that from hence forth on, they would meet as only common and indifferent acquaintances.

Chapter 9

Georgiana had breakfast sent up on a tray to her room, hesitant to face her brother and sister at the breakfast table with red-rimmed eyes. Eventually she would have to come out of her room for a series of dress fittings, but until then she desired some privacy, exhausted as she was by the social exertions of the night before.

The maid that returned to retrieve her tray shot a look of dismay at her back upon surveying the amount of food still left. The Master and the Mistress would not be pleased.

Georgiana purposefully avoided eye contact with the maid upon her arrival, knowing what her response would be to the remnants on the tray. She was relieved to hear the click of the door as it closed behind her, although she was well aware that the maid would no doubt be reporting her observation to Mrs. Cole, who would in turn inform Elizabeth. She could only hope that Elizabeth would choose to keep the information from her brother.

There was a reasonable chance that Elizabeth would put it down to her excuse of a headache the night before, but her sister could be very discerning when she chose to be. She seated herself in front of her dressing table with a sigh and splashed some cool water on her face to help erase the effects of her long night. She only wished that the pain in her heart could be erased so easily.

*****

She emerged from her room sometime later looking somewhat worse for wear, but considerably less so than when she had gotten out of bed that morning. She paused to check her appearance one more time in a mirror outside the drawing room. She patted her hair, checking the stability of her simple up-do, and agonized over the dark circles she had been unable to conceal under her eyes.

There was nothing more she could do before facing Elizabeth. She took a deep breath and smiled stiffly at the footman, who waited for her nod before opening the door and admitting her to the drawing room.

She entered the room to find Elizabeth in the midst of a dress fitting, the dressmaker's assistant kneeling at her feet, pins stuck out of her mouth. Her sister glanced at her with a warm smile.

"Good morning, Georgiana. I hope you are feeling better this morning," Elizabeth said, without moving.

Georgiana smiled wanly as she made her way to an empty chair to wait her turn. "I am, thank you."

Elizabeth watched Georgiana from the corner of her eye as she fidgeted in her seat, observing her tired visage and subdued nature. Between her sister's actions the night before and her avoidance of the breakfast table that morning, combined with her current appearance, she had the inkling that something had gone very wrong the night before. Wisely though, she chose to remain silent on the subject, instead introducing a more soothing topic.

"Your brother found some sheet music yesterday he thought you might be interested in," Elizabeth stated, hoping to get some sort of reaction from her preoccupied sister.

"Oh, that's nice," Georgiana replied, distracted.

"He also thought you might enjoy going to the opera tomorrow evening," she tried again.

Georgiana did perk up a little at the mention of the opera. Her reticent brother preferred to stay away from the crowds surrounding the opera house. Very rarely did she have the opportunity to attend, even when she was in Town.

"Oh, he did? What is playing?" she asked.

"Elisabetta regina d'Inghilterra, by Gioachino Rossini," Elizabeth replied. "Are you interested in seeing it? It has only just opened."

She thought briefly upon the matter; Rossini was not as much a favorite of hers as Mozart was, but Mozart's influence was easily discernible in his compositions. The story was a pleasant one and the music promised to be delightful. She answered in the affirmative.

Elizabeth could only be pleased with the outcome, and did not press her further.

*****

When Georgiana stepped out of the carriage that night in front of the King's Theatre she was overawed by the splendor that surrounded her. It seemed that all of London had turned out for the night. Men and women were dressed in their best finery, jewels glittering, feathers swaying amidst the crush of people. Gas lights lit the streets, casting a flickering glow over the swarming mass of people trying to make their way in.

Darcy was uncomfortable with the throngs around them. He firmly tucked Georgiana's hand around one arm and Elizabeth's around the other.

"Do not allow yourself to become separated from me," he warned them firmly. "I will never find you in the midst of all these people."

Georgiana had no desire to tempt her brother's protective instincts under the circumstances. Even Elizabeth, with her normal penchant for independence, seemed overwhelmed as she clung tightly to her husband's arm. They were far from the peace and solitude of Pemberley.

It was with much relief that Darcy was able to deposit them at their box sometime later. Georgiana could see him visibly relax as he pulled the velvet curtains closed, signally that there would be no visitors to their box.

Curiously, she looked across the way at the boxes facing them. With a jolt, she realized that the Rycroft family occupied the box almost directly across from them, and Miranda Rycroft had her opera glasses trained on their box. As she watched, she was even more astonished to see the Crosbys, including Thaddeus, join them. Miranda immediately sat down her glasses to welcome the newcomers, steering Thaddeus into the seat next to hers.

At that moment, the lights dimmed, signaling the start of the production, and Georgiana was forced to turn her attention toward the stage to try and concentrate on the performance.

*****

Thaddeus spent most of the first act annoyed by the constant interruptions of Miss Rycroft as she tried to distract his attention from the performance to herself.

He couldn't believe he had allowed Caroline to convince him to come tonight. If he'd known that they would be joining her little "friend's" family in their box, he most certainly would have refused. Her obnoxious behavior toward him was bordering on improper and he could only be glad that Georgiana wasn't there to witness it.

He'd had enough of her over-familiarity, false flattery, and scheming to last him a lifetime. If he could remain polite just long enough to get through tonight, then he would do all in his power to avoid being thrown together with her at any subsequent events. If he had to take a page out of Darcy's book and refuse to dance with her, he would.

He could only hope that Miranda's constant insinuations had not reached Georgiana, but there was not much chance of that.

After much thought on the evening before, he had realized Georgiana's behavior towards him had changed after she spoke with Miranda and had only continued to go downhill after supper. He could only conclude that she must have said something to make Georgiana doubt his affections.

He had only to suffer through tonight, and then on the morrow he would call and set about making amends- if Georgiana would see him. He desperately hoped she would.

When the curtain dropped at the close of the first act for intermission, Thaddeus' first thought was to escape the box with the excuse of fetching some refreshments. He would do almost anything to get himself out of Miranda's clutches.

He glanced at her, about to ask if she would like anything, and noticed that her gaze was caught by someone across the way. He followed her line of sight and was horrified to see the Darcys seated in the box directly across from them. He froze in his seat, hoping against hope that Georgian hadn't noticed them.

He had been led to believe the Darcys avoided the opera. The crowds certainly held little appeal to him, and he could only think that Darcy would feel the same. But he should have known that Georgiana, with her love of music, would convince her brother to take her to see the new production of Elisabetta regina d'Inghilterra. The man did not have it in him to disappoint his sister.

As he watched, Georgiana's gaze slowly swung in his direction, until their eyes met across the expanse of the auditorium. His heart sank. He gave a small nod in her direction, acknowledging that he had seen her, and she returned the gesture.

No longer caring what his companions thought or if they desired any refreshments, he rose and excused himself from the box, intent on making his way to the Darcys' box. He had no idea what he would say or do when he got there, but he couldn't seem to help it. He was drawn to her.

*****

Georgiana was surprised by Thaddeus' abrupt departure from the box, but she assumed that he had gone to retrieve refreshments for the ladies of his party. *He would probably do anything for Miranda,* she thought bitterly, forgetting momentarily her resolution to view him only as an indifferent acquaintance.

How wrong she was. It took Thaddeus quite some time to snake his way through the throngs to the Darcy's box. He was stopped several times by acquaintances wishing to involve him in some mundane chit-chat, but he persevered until, finally, he found himself before their box.

The heavy curtains had only been parted slightly to allow for visitors, and Darcy had posted himself just outside, drink in hand. He looked very much as if he were guarding his ladies from any unwanted company.

Thaddeus was slightly taken aback by Darcy's stance, but he was undeterred from his goal.

"Good to see you, Darcy," he greeted him. "I was surprised to find you in attendance tonight. I would have thought you'd prefer to avoid the crowds."

Darcy harrumphed. "Yes, well, my wife and sister had a sudden desire to see this new production. I couldn't very well allow them to attend alone."

"No, of course not," Thaddeus conceded. "Are they inside? I'd very much like to pay my respects if I may."

Darcy gestured him inside, unaware, as men sometimes are, that anything might be wrong. "I'm sure they would be most pleased to see you." He followed Thaddeus through the curtain.

The women had heard the sound of voices through the curtain and had turned expectantly in their seats to greet their guest. Elizabeth greeted Thaddeus with a gentle smile and a knowing gleam in her eye. Here at least, he had an accomplice in his endeavors and a knowledgeable source.

Georgiana on the other hand, greeted him in a decidedly cool manner. She was polite, but void of emotion. It was almost as if there had never been anything between them, as if they were meeting only as acquaintances. He found this thought to be even more troubling than her distinct discomfiture with him of the night before.

Did she have no feeling toward him? What had happened between one day and the next to bring about this change in attitude? He had expected anger, jealousy, or even suspicion. But this- how was he to respond to this?

He left the box feeling more confused than ever, having resolved nothing other than an intention to call the following morning. Even this intention, once announced, did not bring about any animation in Georgiana. Where once her eyes would have shinned with pleasure and an anticipatory smile would have graced her lips, she had only nodded and expressed a generic platitude- that she would look forward to seeing him on the morrow. He did not know what to make of it.

Perhaps Elizabeth would have some insight into the matter to share with him. She, at least, seemed to approve of him as a suitor for her sister. Hopefully, she would be able to help him out of the predicament he seemed to find himself in towards Georgiana.

The second act passed in a blur for both Georgiana and Thaddeus. Georgiana reflected that she could not even recall half of the performance as she climbed into the carriage afterwards. Her attention to the music had been lost before the musicians had even begun to play.

*****

The gray light of dawn found Thaddeus still awake, gazing blankly into the dying embers of the fire lit in his bedroom grate. He still held the remnants of a forgotten glass of whiskey in his hand and his neglected book sat unopened on the table. It had been his turn for a sleepless night, waiting and watching for the light of day, for the chance to make things right again.

Even as the sun crested the horizon, he knew that there was yet more waiting to come before he could present himself at the Darcy's townhouse.

He took extra care with his toilette that morning. He felt ridiculous, trying on first one waistcoat, then another, before rejecting them both for a third, but he knew the end results were worth it. He insisted his valet retie his cravat ten times, until it fell perfectly below his throat. He spent twice as long styling his hair, coaxing the unruly curls into submissive waves. But when he showed himself into the breakfast room, the empty room testified that it was still far too early.

He filled his plate and sat down at the table with a cup of coffee and the morning paper. He felt a slight twinge in his heart as he shook out the paper, remembering how he and Georgiana had often shared the paper over breakfast at Chetborn. He took his time sipping his coffee and pouring over every inch of the bylines. The food on his plate slowly disappeared until he was down to the last few bites. It was at this point that his brother finally made an appearance at the breakfast table.

"Good morning, Alfred," Thaddeus greeted his brother, glad to have someone to keep him from his own thoughts. "Where is Caroline this morning?"

"She had a tray sent up to her room," Alfred said distractedly as he filled a plate from the sideboard.

Thaddeus allowed his brother to sit down and begin to eat before he spoke further, knowing he was far more likely to gain his attention that way.

"What is on your schedule today?" Thaddeus asked, searching for anything that would get his brother talking and his own mind off his problems.

"Nothing too exciting I'm afraid," Alfred responded, "I've a meeting with my steward and then I've a mind to head down to my club and catch up on the news."

Thaddeus glanced at the paper that he had folded and set beside his plate upon his brother's arrival. "Judging by the paper, I'd say the news in the club won't be terribly stimulating. But I'm sure Caroline would be interested in any gossip you do pick up."

His brother harrumphed but didn't respond, focusing instead on his food.

"What does Caroline have planned for the day?" Thaddeus made another attempt to draw Alfred out.

"Oh, probably some calls and then a little shopping," Alfred responded. "She's been cooped up in the house all of the past week preparing for the ball, so I expect we shan't see much of her for the next few days. Too much lost time socializing to make up for."

Thaddeus couldn't help but heave a sigh of relief at that news. She'd had the entire household in her iron fist in the days leading up to and immediately following the ball, and he was glad to be formally released.

"What are your plans for today?" Alfred asked, surprising Thaddeus with his sudden interest.

"I've a few calls to make myself this morning, and then I have a meeting with my man of business," Thaddeus replied.

"Oh? Are you finishing up the paperwork for that estate up north you've finally decided to purchase?" Alfred inquired.

"Yes. I've just got to sign a few things today so the sale can proceed as planned. If everything goes well, this time next week, I'll be a landowner," Thaddeus responded, with some pride.

"Coming up in the world," Alfred observed with a raised eyebrow. "Those matchmaking mamas will be pleased."

He laughed at the grimace that crossed Thaddeus' face.

"You know very well that I have no intentions of pleasing any of those matchmaking mamas, as you so eloquently called them," he chided his brother.

"I do know," Alfred acknowledged. "But said mamas do not. Watch your back, dear brother. There is no end to the lengths they will go to secure a comfortable life for their daughters."

He regarded Thaddeus soberly before issuing a warning, "And if you have any doubts that Miranda Rycroft would do the same, you are misleading yourself. Be careful. She will trap you if she can. She does not give up easily."

Thaddeus acknowledged the warning with a nod, before rising. "I'm off. Enjoy your day, Brother."

A short while later the butler was admitting him into the Darcy's townhouse. He entered the drawing room with some trepidation, unsure of his reception.

Unfortunately, despite his early arrival, he was not the first guest in the Darcy drawing room. Thaddeus' heart fell when he realized none other than Miranda Rycroft was seated beside Georgiana, talking nonstop. Elizabeth was seated across the room from them, diligently working on some needlework. She looked up upon his entrance and welcomed him with a smile.

Miranda also noticed his arrival. She immediately turned her attention upon him as he stood wavering in the doorway. Georgiana's eyes flicked between Miranda and Thaddeus. Briefly, they connected with his gaze, filled with such a deep longing that his heart ached with the need to reassure her that he still loved her.

She quickly transferred her gaze to rest on her clasped hands, but it was too late. She had revealed herself enough for Thaddeus to be reassured that his feelings were still returned. She could not hide behind the Darcy mask forever. His hopes rose again; his determination was renewed. They would get through this.

"Hello Mr. Crosby! What a delight to see you again!" Miranda exclaimed. "I was just going to call on Caroline to deliver an invitation to my family's ball this next week." She started to half-rise from her seat and Thaddeus made a snap decision, seating himself beside Elizabeth before she could make her way to him.

Across the room, Miranda had no choice but to return to her conversation with Georgiana, though she appeared very disgruntled by his actions.

Elizabeth inclined her head toward Thaddeus, smiling mischievously. "Very nicely played, Mr. Crosby. Tell me, what is your game?"

Thaddeus sighed. "There is no game. I am simply trying to find out what happened at the ball and repair the damage. I suspect it has something to do with the conniving Miss Rycroft."

"I suspect you might be correct," Elizabeth responded. "Georgiana has been rather down since the ball, and I think that Miranda told her something to make her think that there was an agreement between you and her."

"I wouldn't put it past her." Thaddeus said, frustrated. "And now I can't get close enough to Georgiana to make things right. Miss Rycroft seems to keep showing up wherever I go."

Elizabeth smiled. "Well, I would be willing to help you, if you would like. Will you be attending the Rycroft's ball?"

Thaddeus sat up a little straighter and a hint of a smile twitched upon his lips as he said, "I had not intended to, but I will make an effort to attend if Georgiana will be. But do you think she'll speak to me?"

"Leave it to me," Elizabeth promised. "I'll see that you're able to speak with her."

The requisite fifteen minutes for the visit being up, Thaddeus rose and bid the ladies good-bye, glad to have an accomplice in Elizabeth and relieved that he was headed to his business man and not the townhouse.

He had no doubt Miranda would be on her way there shortly, triumphant that she had kept him from speaking with Georgiana. But he was hopeful that all would be resolved soon, and then there would be no doubt as to his and Georgiana's future together.

He whistled a jaunty tune as he mounted his horse and guided it through the streets of London.

*****

The morning of the Rycroft's ball dawned bright, the rays of sunlight casting a cheerful glow over everything. Darcy, Elizabeth, and Georgiana were all seated around the breakfast table, enjoying their morning coffee. Georgiana and Darcy were immersed in the paper, while Elizabeth watched them, amused.

A footman appeared at Elizabeth's elbow bearing the morning post. He bowed and offered her a letter off the top of the stack. "For you, madam."

He laid the rest of the bundle beside Darcy's plate, as the master was far too deep in the paper to take notice. Elizabeth's eyes eagerly scanned the address, and her eyes lit up as she recognized the handwriting.

"It's from Jane!" she exclaimed.

Darcy merely grunted noncommittally in response, but Georgiana looked up from her paper with a smile.

"Oh, I do hope it is good news," she said as Elizabeth opened the letter and began pouring over its contents.

Elizabeth paused midway through the letter to squeal, drawing even her husband's attention. "It's a girl! She's had a girl! Eliza Rosalind Bingley. She writes: 'I know you've never cared for the name yourself, Lizzie, but we wanted to name her for you and yet still allow her to have her own unique identity attached to her name. She is the perfect baby, but I know that every mother must feel the same about their child.'"

She paused to read further before adding with a laugh, "She says that Geoffrey is quite repulsed by the baby. Apparently she spit up on him when he first tried to hold her and now he won't come near her. On the bright side, he is actually beginning to behave in order to attract his parent's attention."

She read on, and Georgiana and Darcy waited expectantly for her to finish, both anticipating what was to come. Darcy looked through the letters that had been set beside his plate while he waited. When she came to the end, she addressed her husband and sister, "She asks if Georgiana and I would attend her during her confinement. She says she knows it is a terrible inconvenience, but that she wishes desperately for some companionship. What do you think?"

Darcy held up a letter he had set aside. "I believe I have a plea here from Bingley asking for the very same thing. You know I could never keep you from your sister, darling. Go to her. She will need you, especially with young Geoffrey running around with no one but Nurse to make him mind."

"What about you Georgiana?" Elizabeth asked. "Would you be willing to go?"

The younger woman took a moment to collect her thoughts, setting aside her napkin and paper to buy time.

"I believe I should like to go," she said slowly. Then gaining confidence she added, "Yes, I should very much like to."

Her heart was torn, but her resolve was firm. Distance would help to heal her broken heart. Here in town, she was reminded daily of Miranda's claims and thrust in company with her and Thaddeus constantly. Why, she had been dreading that very night and the trials it would bring at the Rycroft's ball. It would be better for all concerned if she was no longer around.

Elizabeth was far too excited by the news of her new niece to remember the promises she had made Thaddeus earlier in the week. "We shall leave as soon as the coach can be made ready. Darcy, dear, will you see to it that our baggage follows speedily?" Elizabeth stated firmly, folding her letter and setting it aside.

Her husband nodded. "Give your instructions to the maids and I shall personally escort it to Chetborn. It is on the way home to Pemberley and will be as convenient a resting place as any. Now, you had better send an express to your sister or she will not be expecting you so soon."

Elizabeth agreed, and immediately rose from the table to write the express and begin packing. Georgiana followed more slowly, and Darcy could sense a lingering hesitation in her that he refrained from commenting on. He would allow her the freedom to make her own decisions in life, right or wrong.

A very short while later, the Darcy coach waited at the door for the two Darcy women. Many good-byes were said and hugs and kisses exchanged all around, with promises to see each other in the very near future.

"You'll take good care of the children, won't you?" Elizabeth asked her husband worriedly, some trepidation returning at the thought of leaving her babies.

"You know I will," Darcy reassured her as he held little William. "And Nurse will still be with us to help. Now you had better go or you won't make it to the first inn before nightfall."

Elizabeth stepped closer for a last lingering kiss and a few whispered words of love and endearment before allowing herself to be handed up into the traveling coach. Georgiana followed closely behind her, turning to wave one last time at her brother and his children.

And then they were gone.

*****

Thaddeus waited all night for the Darcy's to arrive at the Rycroft's ball. After dodging Miranda repeatedly, she finally managed to corner him beside the refreshment table.

"Why, Mr. Crosby," she purred, "what a delight to finally be able to speak with you! I feared that we would never have an opportunity to talk with my being in such large demand tonight."

Thaddeus didn't quite know how to respond to such blatant self-proclamation and really had no desire to. He attempted to mutter an unintelligible response and move past her, but she blocked his escape.

"I just had the best piece of news to share with you! I am quite in raptures over it. The Darcys sent a note round this afternoon explaining they would not be able to attend tonight. It seems Mrs. Darcy's sister has had a baby and the ladies have gone off to attend her in her confinement. Isn't that just the best news? I do so love to hear of a baby!" Miranda said, a glint in her eye.

I have no doubt that you are glad to have Georgiana removed from Town, Thaddeus thought bitterly, *One less piece in the game. Well, there is about to be* ***two*** *less.*

He straightened his shoulders and replied, "That is good news. I'm sure Mr. and Mrs. Bingley are to be congratulated. If you will excuse me, I see a friend of mine I'd like to speak to."

He pushed past Miranda, uncaring of the rudeness or impropriety of such an action, leaving her staring at his back open-mouthed. He did not even pretend to seek out the fictional friend, instead immediately collecting his coat and hat and having his horse brought round. The reason he had come tonight was no longer viable. In a way, Miranda had saved him some frustration since there was no further reason for him to wait around. Georgiana would not be there.

He was disappointed, but as he guided his horse into the streets of London a small smile graced his lips. All was not lost. He still had one more ace to play.

*****

The journey to Chetborn was a long and arduous one, especially undertaken in such haste. Georgiana and

Elizabeth arrived dusty and travel-worn, exhausted from the long hours in the coach. Even traveling in as great as comfort as the Darcy fortune allowed for, the road was not an easy one and the best springs could not prevent them from feeling the bumps in the road. It was two very sore and weary women who stepped from the coach and were eagerly ushered inside by Bingley.

Darcy was following only a few days behind, having stayed only long enough to make sure the townhouse was closed up properly and their belongings packed for the trip north. The journey would take him a little longer since he was traveling with two small children, which of itself necessitated more stops. But he was content to go at their pace, as this allowed him to spend time exclusively with them that he would not otherwise be able to enjoy.

About the same time that Georgiana and Elizabeth were arriving at Chetborn, Thaddeus was being shown into his man of business' office.

"Good morning, Mr. Crosby," the man said jovially, as Thaddeus took the seat across from him. "I shan't take up much of your time today. I have the finalized bill of sale and the deed for your new estate."

He handed the paperwork over to Thaddeus. "May I be the first to congratulate you, sir, on your purchase. I think you will be very pleased with Wylington. That part of Derbyshire is very beautiful. When do you intend to take up residence?"

"Immediately."

Chapter 10

Bingley wasted no time showing Elizabeth and Georgiana into his wife's room. Jane looked up from watching her daughter sleep in her arms to greet them with a serene smile.

"I'm so pleased to see you both," she said softly as they approached the bed, leaving Bingley to wait by the door. "Would you like to see my daughter?"

Elizabeth seated herself on the bed and gently folded back the blanket so she could see the baby's face.

"So this is Miss Eliza," Elizabeth murmured. "You've chosen her namesake poorly Jane, for she looks just like you."

"She *is* beautiful," Georgiana contributed, staring bleakly at the little girl while the other two women talked of things that only a mother could understand. Georgiana felt a sudden intense longing for what could have been and now never would be. A few short weeks ago she had been imagining herself in this very position, with her own child in her arms, and Thaddeus nearby as the proud papa.

She was jerked from her thoughts by Elizabeth, asking her a question.

"What was that?" she asked. "I'm afraid I wasn't attending to the conversation."

The two women gave her understanding looks, and Elizabeth repeated her question, "Are you ready to get out of these dusty clothes?"

"Oh, yes please," Georgiana said quickly. "It was a rather long trip. I hope you will excuse our appearance."

"It is my fault, really," Jane replied apologetically, "for I insisted Charles bring you up the minute you arrived. I simply could not wait to introduce you to Eliza."

"Well, we are very glad that you did so," Elizabeth reassured her sister teasingly, "for we have been longing to make her acquaintance. Now though, we really must change. We'll try not to linger."

"Charles will show you to your rooms," Jane acquiesced. "Please do not hurry back on my account. You've had a long journey. You should rest. Now that I know you are here, I shall be able to rest easy." Elizabeth leaned over to hug her sister before they both followed Bingley out of the room.

Both ladies availed themselves of the opportunity to rest after their arduous journey, but Georgiana, after a short while, found herself to be restless now that she was again in the place that held so many memories of her time with Thaddeus. It was bittersweet to think of him here, where her dreams for the future had taken flight.

She was firmly grounded now though, she reminded herself. She took some time to make herself presentable, fixing a few strands of hair that had come loose and straightening her dress. When she finally opened her door to emerge, she was surprised to find someone waiting outside of it.

"Why Geoffrey whatever are you doing here? Where is Nurse?" she asked, crouching down to the young man's level.

He shrugged. "I dunno. Did you know Mama had a baby?"

"Yes, I did know," Georgiana said, confused.

"I have to be quiet so Mama and the baby can rest," he stated, before adding, "I don't think Mama likes me as much as she likes the baby."

"Oh, Geoffrey!" Georgiana said, pulling the little boy into her arms for a hug. "I know your Mama loves you very much. Right now, the baby is very little and it needs your Mama to do things for it that big boys like you don't need help with. That's why she hasn't been spending as much time with you. But now that I'm here, we can play together. Would you like me to read you a story?"

His eyes lit up. "Would you? Mama don't have the time to read anymore."

She stood up and took his hand. "I sure will. Why don't we go pick one out together?" Together, they headed off in the direction of the library.

That night, they were a very informal party as they all took their evening meal on trays in Jane's room, none of them willing to forego the other's company for the pomp of the dining room.

The days passed in similar form. Elizabeth spent much of her time entertaining Jane while Georgiana spent hers keeping Geoffrey out of mischief. Darcy and the children came and went, Thea's company giving Georgiana a brief respite from her almost exclusive attendance upon Geoffrey.

Time passed slowly for Georgiana, but Geoffrey's presence and need for attention kept her mind from what might otherwise have been a very lonely time.

Chapter 11

Darcy walked the streets of Lambton alone for the first time in a very long time. He felt himself to be rather lonely and melancholy with his wife firmly entrenched at Chetborn for the time being. His lively wife never passed up the opportunity to visit the small village where so many memories had been made, and he reminisced wistfully to himself as he trudged along.

Without the calming presence of his wife by his side, he did not engage the passerby in conversation. He chose instead to visit the necessary shops as quickly as possible, not lingering to make small talk. The townspeople recognized his stoic appearance and whispered to themselves that Mrs. Darcy must be out of town for the good Mr. Darcy to be so withdrawn again.

He was preparing to mount his horse and return home when an unexpected voice called his name. He turned in some surprise to greet the man.

"Crosby! What a pleasure to see you here!" he exclaimed. "What brings you to Lambton?"

"You'll remember I was interested an estate nearby, Wylington." He paused for Darcy to answer in the affirmative. "Well, I've bought it. I just came to town to purchase some supplies."

Darcy smiled broadly, shocking all those passing by. "I'm very pleased to hear that you have joined the neighborhood. My wife will be very happy when I write her about this new development."

Thaddeus sighed. "Yes, well it's not all good news. Managing an estate is not as simple as I had stupidly thought it would be. Do you happen to know how I can get myself a new steward? I had to let the last one go after taking a good look at the books. He had been swindling the previous owners and I couldn't in good faith keep him on."

"I might be able to help you," Darcy said seriously as he pondered the younger man's predicament. "Why don't we discuss it over dinner tonight?"

Thaddeus smiled. "I should like that very much."

The two men parted ways, pleased with this latest turn of events.

*****

Thaddeus wound his way through an extensive wood as he traversed the park of Pemberley on his way to the great house itself. He was beginning to despair of reaching the house in time for dinner when he crested a hill and the full splendor of the façade, bathed in sunlight, was before him. He unconsciously pulled back on the reigns, slowing his horse as he took it all in.

He swallowed, intimidated by the sight before him. This was where Georgiana had grown up, in all its magnificence. Here is where she had played in the halls and raced across the lawn as a child; here is where she still sometimes sat beside the stream and read in the library. The townhouse that he had been so in awe of was nothing compared to Pemberley. Wylington, where he hoped to someday bring her as his wife, suddenly seemed very small and dowdy in comparison.

Fighting back a slight panic, he reminded himself that material things were naught to Georgiana. She would be happy with whatever he was able to provide for her, even if it wasn't quite up to the standards of what Darcy could. She knew that as a younger son his portion was not what his brother's was. She would not expect him to go into debt in order to keep her in the style she was accustomed to. She would be happy at Wylington because they would be together, he told himself firmly, even if he only had five thousand pounds per annum and not the rumored ten thousand Darcy did.

He swallowed once more, firmly pushing his anxiety down, and kicked his horse back to a walk. As he neared the entranceway he found himself cast in the imposing structure's shadow. He felt very small and insignificant next to this reminder of the Darcy's importance. He could only be grateful that Georgiana had given him a second glance.

Darcy greeted him in the entryway and led him into a drawing room to wait for dinner to be announced.

"Are Thea and Will here with you?" Thaddeus asked, looking around. "Or they at Chetborn with Mrs. Darcy?"

"They are here," Darcy assured him, "but they've had their supper already in the nursery. Nurse is going to put them to bed for me tonight."

"Oh," Thaddeus said, a little disappointed. He had looked forward to seeing what he hoped would soon be his niece and nephew.

Darcy watched his expression knowingly and offered, "Perhaps the next time you visit I can have them brought down. I know Thea will be very pleased to see you. She often talks about the time we all spent together at Chetborn."

Thaddeus brightened a little. "I'd like that very much." If he couldn't see Georgiana yet, at least he could be with the family she loved so much.

"So, how are you enjoying your new status as a landowner?" Darcy asked, with obvious amusement.

Thaddeus shot Darcy a dark look. "I wish my father had spent as much time teaching me how to run an estate as he did Alfred. It would have made this move much easier. I've been pleased with the performances of most of the servants that worked for the previous owner. But I simply cannot stand having someone around me who would cheat their employer."

He paused as Darcy acknowledged the wisdom of this move before going on, "I wish I had realized at the time how much work a steward does. I've been hunting for a suitable steward since, but right now I have to do all his work on top of my own. It's exhausting and overwhelming. I'm hoping you have some connections I can use to find some help."

"I have some recommendations for a steward," Darcy said, "but if you prefer I can refer you to an agency that will help you find one. However, that route may take a little longer since you will have a lot of correspondence before you ever interview anyone."

"I need someone capable as soon as possible," Thaddeus replied. "Who do you recommend?"

Just then, dinner was announced, and Darcy led the way out of the drawing room saying, "Why don't we discuss that over dinner?"

By the time dinner concluded, Thaddeus had several recommendations of local men to consider and the two men had agreed to meet the next day so Darcy could look over Wylington with Thaddeus and make suggestions.

As the men enjoyed their port, Thaddeus broached another topic, one more dear to his heart.

He swirled the port in his glass, keeping his gaze downward as he asked, "So how is Miss Darcy?"

Normally, he would hesitate to ask, but Darcy knew the intentions he had toward Georgiana, and he had already taken steps to follow through with them by moving to Derbyshire. There was no reason to hide how he felt.

"She's doing fine, as far as I know," Darcy said slowly, not sure how to reply. "Elizabeth writes that she has been spending most of her time with Geoffrey, trying to keep him entertained while Jane cares for the baby."

"That's good," Thaddeus said, searching for something, anything, else to say to prolong the topic.

Darcy took pity on him and added, "Elizabeth did mention that she has occasionally found Georgiana in the library, just staring off into space and that she has been unusually quiet." He paused before hinting, "Perhaps it is due to the circumstances that preceded her removal to Chetborn."

Thaddeus sighed, acknowledging that it was probably so. "I wish I had had the opportunity for us to reach an understanding before she left, but I could never get rid of that obnoxious Miss Rycroft! Whenever she wasn't throwing herself at me, my sister Caroline was trying to throw us together. I will be very pleased to quit the marriage mart for good."

Darcy nodded. "I well remember the feeling."

The two men fell silent. When Thaddeus left that night, he was relieved to know that he would have some help adjusting to his new role, but he was anxious to move forward. He hated this in-between stage, waiting for Georgiana to return, waiting for the time when his life could go on, when things wouldn't be so difficult.

Things could only get better from here.

*****

A few weeks into Jane's confinement found Georgiana in the sitting room, deep in thought under the pretense of attending to some minor mending, while Elizabeth entertained Jane in her room. Geoffrey was under the care of his nurse, giving Georgiana a much needed respite from his enthusiasm.

Footsteps in the hallway drew Georgiana from her reverie. She waited expectantly for them to pass the room, assuming it was a servant performing their duties. But they did not go on. They stopped, directly outside the door.

Curious, she set aside the mending that had lain forgotten in her lap. The footman opened the door to admit a young man, probably in his late twenties, with Adonis good looks and a flattering smile. She rose politely at his entrance.

"Mr. Pierce Aldridge, miss, of Farlewood Hall," the footman announced, monotonously, then resumed his position by the door, leaving it suspiciously open.

The young man drew closer, bowing over the hand she offered and pressing a lingering kiss upon it before asking, "It is a pleasure to make you acquaintance, Miss…?"

She snatched her hand away as demurely as possible before seating herself and taking up the embroidery she had cast aside to prevent any repetition of the act.

"I am Miss Darcy of Pemberley," she said stiffly as he made himself comfortable in a nearby chair. "My sister, Mrs. Darcy, is Mrs. Bingley's sister."

Georgiana felt acutely the impropriety of receiving the unknown young man alone and could not help but be grateful for the open door.

"I can call for my sister to come down so she can receive you," Georgiana offered, hopefully.

"No," Mr. Aldridge dismissed her suggestion. "I would not dream of inconveniencing her. I have just come to offer congratulations on behalf of my family and myself. We live in the neighborhood, you see."

"Oh, I am happy to accept them on the behalf of Mrs. Bingley," Georgiana said, not sure how to respond. "I shall inform her that you came to visit. I regret that we shall not have the pleasure of your mother and sisters' company."

"I'm sure you will see them shortly." He waved this off. "For they are quite the social butterflies, flitting here and there to events. Sadly though, they have all come down with a terrible cold and since my father cannot be torn away from matters of the estate, it fell to me to make the visit."

He smiled wolfishly and ran an appraising look over Georgiana. "I am glad now that the lot fell to me. I cannot say I am disappointed by the results."

She shivered involuntarily under his hungry gaze. Thankfully, her salvation came in the form of Mr. Bingley who, while happening to be passing by, heard voices coming from the sitting room and decided to investigate.

Georgiana had never been so relieved to see someone enter a room as she was to see Charles Bingley's jovial face. His face darkened upon observing who she was entertaining.

Mr. Aldridge rose and bowed a formal greeting to the man of the house, which Bingley acknowledged with a stiff nod.

"Mr. Aldridge," he said in clipped tones, "what a pleasure to see you. I see you have made yourself acquainted with Miss Darcy."

"Yes," the young man said roguishly, "we were just becoming better acquainted. Do give your wife my congratulations on the new arrival."

"I will do so," Bingley said before turning his attention to Georgiana. "Georgiana, your sister was asking for you. If it is of no inconvenience I suggest you attend her now."

Georgiana took the offered out with no further ado, standing and making her curtsey to the two gentleman. She did not offer her hand for any further bestowments.

Later that evening, Bingley pulled her aside to offer a warning.

"Miss Darcy, I normally would not take this duty upon myself, but given the absence of your brother, I feel that it is incumbent upon me to advise you about Mr. Aldridge. He is accounted a rake and a scoundrel and I would heartily suggest that you do not attach yourself to him, nor allow yourself to be present with him in the same room alone." He paused for breath and eyed her seriously. "I cannot prevent him from visiting Chetborn or seeking you out while upon its grounds without good reason, but if ever you have need of my presence do not hesitate to ask."

Georgiana nodded mutely, having no words to respond. Given the short visit that afternoon, she had resolved to avoid the man's company, while assuming that it would not be difficult to do so since she would not be attending any social functions during her stay. She could only hope that, after such a dire warning, Mr. Aldridge would not be as persistent a menace as Mr. Bingley seemed to think he would be.

She was wrong.

The next morning dawned bright and fair, and Georgiana found herself drawn to the gardens as soon as breakfast was finished. While she would have enjoyed the opportunity to wander the grounds on such a fine day, she resigned herself to staying within the confines of the garden in case her sister or Mrs. Bingley needed her services.

She had brought a basket and a pair of shears with her to gather some blooms for the house and she happily set about snipping. Absorbed as she was in the activity, she did not notice she had company in the garden until a voice called out to her, startling her enough that she jerked her hand out of the rose bush and caught her sleeve on a thorn. She briefly inspected the tear, annoyance welling up at the inconvenience, before she got to her feet reluctantly to greet the gentleman.

"Mr. Aldridge," she said, irritation at his appearance and the interruption evident in her voice, "I'm surprised to see you at Chetborn so soon after your visit yesterday. I assure you there are no further congratulations in order."

The man laughed and came to stand beside her, choosing to ignore her comments. "Alas, I am come on business today, not pleasure. My father had some matters to discuss with Mr. Bingley about the local village and he required that I accompany him to observe."

Georgiana tried to maintain a polite tone with the abhorrent gentleman, who was overtly eyeing her figure as he spoke. "You must have lost your way, Mr. Aldridge, as you seem to have found the gardens and not Mr. Bingley's study. I shall find a servant to direct you at once." She made to move to find said servant, but he stopped her with a hand on her arm.

"That is not necessary, Miss Darcy," he assured her. "My father has completed the discussions he wished me to observe and so has released me to find pleasanter company."

She gritted her teeth at being said 'pleasanter company' and turned away to pick up her basket, withdrawing her arm from under his hand at the same time.

"I am afraid you will not find me to be very pleasant company," Georgiana informed him, "as I am quite intent on gathering as many blooms as I can to freshen up the house. I am quite busy, as you can see." She hefted the almost full basket on to her arm to attest to this and held her shears defensively in her other hand so as to ensure there would be no repeat of the inappropriate gesture.

Mr. Aldridge eyed the shears she held in her hand somewhat distractedly as he replied, "Female companionship is always preferable after such tedious tasks. I assure you that I will not be disappointed to accompany you."

Georgiana sighed at his deliberate misinterpretation and moved down the walk to snip some more blooms, resigned to his further company.

She endured his companionship for some time longer, replying shortly to his endless prattle, until his father finally collected him for the trip home.

Georgiana was able to enjoy a brief respite from his attentions for several days before the young Miss Aldridges came to visit, with their brother to accompany them. Thankfully, this time the drawing room was occupied by both Georgiana and Elizabeth upon their arrival, but even this could not dissuade Mr. Aldridge from singling Georgiana out for his particular attentions.

It soon became apparent that the Aldridges had come with a purpose, to invite the current residents of Chetborn to a small card party to be held at Farlewood Hall the following Tuesday.

When they finally left, Georgiana was emotionally worn from the demands of maintaining her polite visage among such trying company. She knew Elizabeth would want to discuss the invitation right away, but she turned pleading eyes on her sister, and the sympathetic older woman granted her a reprieve.

"We can discuss the invitation with Charles and Jane over dinner," she acquiesced, sending a relieved Georgiana out of the room.

Dinner conversation that night was lively as Georgiana argued adamantly against going and Elizabeth and Jane insisted that it was only the proper and neighborly thing to do, especially as Jane would not be able to attend due to her confinement. With her sweet-natured temper, she could not conceive of Mr. Aldridge acting with any impropriety. Elizabeth, for her part, reasoned that she and Charles would be there to support and protect Georgiana from any unwanted advances. Bingley leaned toward agreeing with Georgiana because of his suspicions toward Mr. Aldridge, but could not bring himself to outright disagree with his wife.

In the end, it was agreed that they would attend, largely in part because it was obvious that the lengthy argument had worn Jane out in her weakened state, and no one had any desire to try her further.

It was with great reluctance that Georgiana emerged from the carriage that night and allowed herself to be handed down after Elizabeth. She immediately latched on to Mr. Bingley's arm for support. They were shown into a small parlor that held the family and a few neighboring guests.

Georgiana was glad to find that she was acquainted with all those present, as many of the neighbors had presented themselves at Chetborn to offer their congratulations on the new addition to the family.

The young Miss Aldridges rose excitedly upon their entrance and came to greet her enthusiastically, forcing her to let go of Charles' arm briefly.

That brief moment was all it took to separate her from him as the young ladies quickly pressed her into joining them on the settee and inundated her with all the latest gossip about people she was not acquainted with.

The two chatty young ladies reminded her frighteningly of Lydia Wickham, Elizabeth's younger sister. She had only been in company with the young Mrs. Wickham a handful of times, but her flighty, flirtatious ways had not endeared her to her. Georgiana felt she would go mad, listening to their inane gossip and unable to get a word in edgewise in order to change the subject. Even a frivolous conversation of bonnets or dress styles would be preferable to this.

At length, she was able to extricate herself with the excuse of procuring refreshments, but even this reprieve did not last long.

She had just poured herself a glass of ratafia when an unwelcome acquaintance appeared by her side.

"Good evening, Miss Darcy," Mr. Aldridge greeted her, pouring himself a drink. "I am so pleased that you and your party were able to join us this evening."

Until now, Georgiana had been able to maintain her distance from the young man as he had been engrossed in a high stakes contest with several other young men from the area and thus had been prevented from attending her as she had been held hostage by his sisters.

"Mr. Aldridge," she responded grudgingly.

Flushed with victory at the tables and too much wine, he offered, "I noticed you have not yet participated in any of the card games. You must allow me to find you a place at one of the tables. It is prodigious fun!"

"Thank you, but no," Georgiana replied firmly. "I do not enjoy games of chance."

"Perhaps a game of chess then?" Mr. Aldridge suggested.

Georgiana saw the suggestion for what it was, an attempt to monopolize her attention, as had been the offer before it. She declined firmly once more and excused herself to join her sister, who was speaking with a cluster of young matrons along one wall.

The young man would not be dissuaded so easily, and again sought her out later in the evening. He was more successful this time, as Elizabeth had left her alone on the settee to refill her drink.

He joined her there, and with all the self-satisfaction of a young buck assured of a ready and willing reception, proceeded to regale her with an accounting of the trip he was to embark upon to London the next day.

In the end, she was glad for the accounting, for it provided her with the reassurance that he would not be a bother any longer. Still, she was never so glad to hear the carriage called for as she was at the end of that night.

*****

Back at Pemberley, Darcy received a very disquieting letter from his wife. Thaddeus noticed his distraction as they rode out together to inspect the fields upon his new property.

"What has got you distracted so, Darcy?" Thaddeus asked.

Darcy hesitated to answer, knowing the effect it would have on the other man. He sighed; there was no sense in keeping it from him.

"I received a letter from my wife this morning," he said. "It contained some disturbing news. Apparently, one of the neighboring gentlemen has taken quite an interest in Georgiana."

Thaddeus froze in his seat, not sure how to process the statement.

"She writes that Bingley has some reservations about the fellow and is keeping a close eye upon Georgiana, but I can't help but feel that I should be there," Darcy admitted.

"Has he threatened her in anyway?" Thaddeus said angrily, finding his voice again.

"Not that she writes," Darcy answered. "I wish I knew more of the situation. But I do not, and I can only trust that Bingley will keep things well in hand and not allow his good-natured personality to overrule his gut reaction. In any account, they are due to arrive home in a few days, so hopefully this will all amount to nothing."

Thaddeus was disgruntled by his lack of action and could only wish that he had the right to ride to her side and offer his protection. But he did not. His only option was to stand by helplessly and hope that thirty miles away the love of his life was okay.

*****

Georgiana was inordinately pleased the next morning to be able to rise and enjoy the solitude of the sitting room without the expectation of unwanted company. She settled herself in after the morning meal to work on some embroidery and bask in the light that streamed through the windows. The empty room was a soothing salve for her strained nerves.

It was with some surprise then that Georgiana looked up from her embroidery as Mr. Aldridge was announced. She rose belatedly, confusion evident upon her face. The door was again left conspicuously open, but this did not dissuade the passionate young man.

He took the seat next to Georgiana on the settee, and she immediately regretted not having chosen a chair to sit in.

"Mr. Aldridge!" she exclaimed, still standing. "What a surprise to see you! I did not expect you to visit today."

She began edging toward the door. "Let me just call for Mr. Bingley."

His hand shot out, wrapping itself in a vise-like grip around her wrist.

"No, Miss Darcy," he said plaintively, "we have no need of Mr. Bingley. I have come today to see *you*."

"That is very flattering, sir," Georgiana said firmly, "but I would feel much more comfortable with Mr. Bingley present." She took one more step towards the door, thinking he would release her hand upon her insistence.

Instead, his grip tightened. Passionately, he flung himself to his knees at her feet.

"In vain I have struggled!" he declared, with all the self-assurance only a young man who has never been refused anything can express. "My feelings will not be repressed. You must allow me to tell you how ardently I admire you! From the first moment of my acquaintance with you, your manners and your beauty were such to form the groundwork on which succeeding events have built so immovable an affection as to convince me that you are the only woman in the world whom I could ever be prevailed upon to marry!"

Here his demeanor changed as his ardor got the best of him. He stood and pulled her roughly towards him, eliciting a small cry on her part. She struggled to break free from his grasp, but he held her firmly by the forearms.

"Mr. Aldridge! You are too hasty, sir!" she cried, still struggling. "You forget that I have made no answer."

"There is no need of one," he responded, with all the arrogance of a young man used to getting his way. "I know that you will not deny me."

He leaned in closer, releasing one of her hands to touch a flaxen curl. His eyes focused on her lips, which had compressed into a tight line, and missed the clenched fist she raised.

She punched him square in the nose, with all the force and anger she could muster. He dropped his grip on her to clutch his face, his eyes widening in shock at the blood that dripped between his fingers.

She fled to the doorway, pausing only to inform him with haughty derision, "Let me enlighten you as to my answer without any further loss of time. From the moment of *my* acquaintance with you, your manners, arrogance, conceit, and your selfish disdain of the feelings of others convinced me that you were the last man in the world whom I could ever be prevailed upon to marry."

She did not wait around to see his reaction. She gathered her skirts and ran through the halls and up the stairs as soon as she was out of his line of sight, her hand still throbbing. She made a beeline for Bingley's study.

She burst in upon him in a meeting with his steward. Bingley took one look at her harried appearance and came around the desk to guide her to a chair. She was shaking so violently that he half expected her to collapse at any moment.

"What happened?" he asked worriedly. "Are you all right?"

"Aldridge…proposed…grabbed me…" She brokenly tried to tell the tale, sucking in large gulps of air, "tried to kiss me…"

"Aldridge! Aldridge is here?!" Bingley broke in on her.

She nodded mutely, still trying to catch her breath. He let out a growl under his breath and turned to his steward.

"I want that man out of my house this instant! And he is never to be allowed admittance again!" He fairly shouted at the startled servant, who had never seen his master behave in such a manner. The man scuttled off to see his order carried out.

Bingley turned back to Georgiana and gentled his tone, "Now tell me again what happened."

At that moment, Elizabeth entered through the door the steward had left open in his haste.

"What is going on?" she asked, having noticed the commotion in the house. "The servants are in an uproar!" She took in Georgiana's bedraggled appearance and immediately set herself beside her, pulling the younger woman into her arms.

"Oh my! What happened, dear?" she asked. Tears pooled in Georgiana's eyes at the maternal gesture and she very nearly lost her composure right then and there. She wrapped her arms around Elizabeth and told the story.

By the end of it, Elizabeth's mouth was set in a determined line and Bingley's hands were clenched into fists. Georgiana sat with her eyes downcast, her cheeks wet with tears.

"What is to be done now?" Elizabeth finally asked.

Bingley sighed, most of his anger spent. "I've already had him removed from the premises, and he will never be allowed to return. I had nothing to verify my intuition with before, but I will not allow such a man near my daughter or any other guests of mine."

He steepled his hands together and leaned back in his chair. "I suggest that you and Georgiana return to Pemberley as soon as possible. Your visit was almost to its conclusion anyway. Jane is doing well, and I suspect, while she will miss your company, she will be just fine without you here. And unless I miss my mark, I would assume that Georgiana would welcome the security of home right now."

Georgiana nodded; suddenly more than anything, she wanted to be home at Pemberley with those she loved.

"I don't expect him to try to make any further advances," Bingley went on to say. "He has some gambling debts that, if they fell into the wrong hands, could land him in debtors' prison. I will make it quite clear if he tries anything more I will ruin him. You will be safe from him."

"Very well," Elizabeth responded approvingly. "I had not thought you had it in you, Charles. Darcy would be proud. Now, if you will excuse us, I believe we have some packing to do if we are to depart on the morrow."

Bingley nodded, and the two women left, both eager for their own reasons to return to Pemberley. Elizabeth was impatient to be reunited with her children and husband. The six weeks she had been apart from them had seemed agonizingly long, however much she adored her sister and her new niece.

Georgiana longed for the peace and tranquility she found at Pemberley. Her heart had healed somewhat from the hurt it had suffered at Miranda's hands, but now there was this new trauma to put behind her.

Georgiana and Elizabeth were up very early the next morning, packed and ready to go. Jane was even allowed downstairs to say good-bye, and while they were seen off with smiling faces, there was a silent seriousness that hung over them all.

Geoffrey asked Georgiana very solemnly, "You won't forget me, will you? You'll come back and play with me, right?"

Georgiana hugged the little boy. "Of course I will, Geoffrey. Next time I'll bring Thea for you to play with, too. And maybe if you are a good boy your Mama and Papa will bring you to see me at Pemberley sometime soon."

"That sounds nice," he said seriously, before his eyes lit up. "Then I could ride Thea's pony!"

Georgiana laughed. "Yes, if your parents allow it." She gave him a final parting hug and allowed herself to be handed up into the coach, followed closely by Elizabeth. They were both relieved to be finally underway.

It was a long day's journey home. Despite the early hour in which they had left, it was late in the day when they arrived home. As their arrival was unexpected, they were met at the door by only the butler and Mrs. Reynolds.

Georgiana was exhausted both physically and emotionally. She was covered in dust from the road, sore from the bumpy ride and cramped quarters, and weary after a sleepless night. Elizabeth was doing only slightly better.

Darcy and Thaddeus were sequestered in his study going over crop rotation methods when they heard a commotion in the hallway. Darcy rose from behind his desk and poked his head out the door, hoping to derive some information from the servants bustling through the halls.

"Excuse me," he called out good-humoredly. "You there, Mary is it? Would you care to inform me what the hullabaloo is all about?"

The maid dipped a quick curtsey, flustered to be called out so by the master of the house. "The Mistress is home, sir, and Miss Georgiana."

Darcy cocked his head. "Are you sure? She's not due home for three days yet."

"Yes, sir, it's sure I am."

"Well, then. Thank you, Mary. You may go now," Darcy dismissed her. A smile flittered around Darcy's lips as he turned back into the room.

"Come along now, Crosby. Seems that Elizabeth and Georgiana have returned early," Darcy said jovially, excited to see his wife.

Thaddeus followed Darcy into the entryway, lagging a little behind. As excited as he was to see Georgiana again after six weeks, he was unsure of his reception since they had not parted under the best of circumstances.

Darcy gave his sister an obligatory hug and then went directly to his wife for a long embrace. Georgiana did not immediately notice Thaddeus following in Darcy's wake. Instead, she looked on with a tired smile as her brother held his wife tightly.

The sound of Thaddeus clearing his throat finally drew her attention. She turned towards him with a smile, which froze upon her lips as she recognized him. Her lips formed his name, and he watched as a myriad of emotions crossed her face.

Georgiana was overwhelmed by the crush of emotions she felt upon seeing Thaddeus' hesitant smile. As exhausted as she was, it was all too much for her to deal with. After a brief moment of shock, she burst into tears and fled up the stairs.

Thaddeus took a step back, startled by her reaction. He looked at Darcy and Elizabeth in confusion, hoping there was some explanation.

"Oh dear," Elizabeth said, surfacing from Darcy's embrace at the sudden movement. "I'm afraid she's had a rough few days. I'd better go to her." She hurried off after Georgiana, but turned back to quickly extend an invitation, "I have no idea what is on the menu, but I do hope you will stay for dinner Mr. Crosby."

With no further explanation, the men were left standing in the entry, confusion written on their faces.

*****

Elizabeth knocked gently on Georgiana's suite door.

"Georgiana, dear, can I come in please?" she called.

There was a long pause, but finally she heard a rustle from within and Georgiana pulled the door open and peeked out. Elizabeth's heart went out to the younger woman at the sight of her red-rimmed eyes and sniffling nose.

She stepped inside and closed the door behind her before embracing Georgiana. The younger woman melted in her arms.

"What is he doing here?" she whimpered. "He's not supposed to be here."

"You will have to ask him, dear. I was quite surprised to see Mr. Crosby myself," Elizabeth offered.

"I just wanted to come home and rest! I feel like my life has been turned upside down since this winter. I don't know how to feel anymore. I wish I could just hide myself away in the music room and sort this all out!" Georgiana cried.

"I know you need some time to regain your equilibrium," Elizabeth comforted her sister, "but you are home now, and I'm sure that being back at Pemberley will bring you peace."

Georgiana wiped her cheeks as she calmed with her sister's presence. "I know. I just wasn't expecting to see him. Do you think he's engaged to Miranda?"

"We will have to wait to find out," Elizabeth hedged, although she was fairly certain that had never been an option. "I've invited him to stay for dinner. Perhaps we can ask him then."

Georgiana froze. "You've invited him for dinner?" She hadn't expected to have to face him again so soon after her loss of composure.

"Yes," Elizabeth said with a slightly raised eyebrow. "I did not expect you to be so missish."

"No, no, I'm not," Georgiana hastened to reassure her, swallowing hard. "I'm sure that will be lovely."

Elizabeth tucked a strand of hair that had come loose behind Georgiana's ear.

"It will all work out," she reassured gently.

Georgiana sighed. "I wish I had your confidence. You'd better go off to see about dinner arrangements. There's no way of knowing what Fitzwilliam had Mrs. Reynolds order for dinner. I'll just take some time to collect myself, if you don't mind. I promise I won't embarrass Brother so again."

"That will be fine," Elizabeth said. "Don't feel bad, dear. After the last few weeks you've had, your reaction was perfectly natural." She gave Georgiana one last hug before heading out the door. "I'll see you at dinner then."

"Yes, I'll see you then," Georgiana murmured as the door closed behind Elizabeth. She collapsed on to the settee, overwhelmed.

This day would just not end.

Chapter 12

Thaddeus waited anxiously as the time for dinner approached. Darcy had disappeared to talk to his wife, depositing Thaddeus in the library to entertain himself. He supposed he should be grateful for the rather callous treatment since it showed that Darcy was beginning to view him as family and no longer as a guest.

They had grown more comfortable with each other as they had spent the last few weeks in rather close company. They had spent most of their days ensconced in the study pouring over accounts or out riding the boundaries of Thaddeus' new estate. Darcy had been of great help to him as he came to grips with his new responsibilities. He felt almost equipped to handle them now.

Thaddeus stood to pace the room, tugging on his waistcoat. He needed some means to distract himself from this constant, agonizing nervousness. He picked up a book and sat it back down almost as quickly. He brushed imaginary dirt from his jacket. Finally, he admitted defeat and took himself off to the one room in the house where he knew he could find some peace.

The music room had sat unused for some time now, with Georgiana gone first to Town and then to Chetborn. Darcy had pointed it out to him during one of his first visits to Pemberley as one of Georgiana's favorite rooms in the house. He had always somehow felt closer to her there, as if she would somehow materialize at the pianoforte.

He sat down at the instrument and was surprised to find a piece of dog-eared, well worn sheet music already on the stand. He smiled as he recognized the piece. Mozart. The one she had played so long ago at Chetborn, and then again at the townhouse in London.

He set his fingers on the keys and began to pick out the tune.

In her quarters, Georgiana recognized the music as it filtered to her through the hallways and doors. Who could be playing? Elizabeth would not attempt such a complicated piece, nor was she likely to play without being called upon in company to do so. As she had once told Lady Catherine, she could not be prevailed upon to practice.

Intrigued, she allowed herself to be drawn from the security of her room. She padded softly through the hallways, following the melody until she reached the music room. She peeked around the door and was surprised to see Thaddeus at the instrument. She blushed to realize that he must have found the piece on the stand where she had left it.

He was concentrating far too hard on the sheet music to notice her spying on him. She listened awhile longer. While he lacked the finesse she had acquired with years of practice, he did the piece justice with his playing. His offer of a duet had not been an idle one.

His gaze turned wistful under her watchful eyes as he came upon a familiar part of the melody. Watching him, she could not help but feel that there was still something between them. He would not have chosen that piece, *their song,* if he did not long for their former connection as she did.

She did not know what the story was with Miranda, and she was still somewhat cautious after her run-in with Mr. Aldridge the day before, but she would hear him out. Some of her confusion started to fade away.

She returned to her room to prepare for dinner, finally feeling a measure of peace.

*****

Thaddeus let the last few notes linger, drawing them out until they were only faint echoes in the room. As they faded away, he withdrew his fingers from the keys and sighed. If only he could revive their relationship as easily.

Still, he felt closer to her, just by being here, in her special place. She let the true depth of her feelings and emotions show when she was at the pianoforte, and never more so than when she was at home with her family. She did not hide behind an expressionless mask like she did in company. She was warm and passionate. He felt privileged to have been able to see Georgiana in a light that few ever would.

He suddenly became aware of the darkening room and realized that dinner must be almost upon them. Who knows how long he had sat there woolgathering! He stood and ran his fingers lovingly over the ivory keys one last time before he shut the lid over them. He cast one final glance at the music on the stand before he turned away, leaving it as he had found it.

*****

Elizabeth and Darcy were far too deep in conversation to notice the music that filtered through Pemberley. Darcy was seated on his wife's bed, already changed for dinner, watching as her lady's maid coaxed her unruly curls into subjection. He knew better than to ask for an explanation for Georgiana's earlier behavior while there was a servant present. He was waiting as patiently as he could for his wife to finish dressing so he could get some answers to his questions.

Elizabeth raised her eyebrow sardonically at her husband's steady gaze in the mirror. She well knew the questions on his mind and the impatience he was trying to suppress. Still, she couldn't resist teasing her husband a little.

"Alice, can you curl these ringlets a little more? They look a little loose," she said seriously, although she couldn't hide the twinkle in her eye.

Alice, of course, was eager to please her mistress and quickly moved to redo the curls. Darcy's eyes darkened and his brows furrowed at the further delay. Elizabeth couldn't help but enjoy his disgruntled attitude, but in the end, she took pity on him.

"Thank you, Alice," she said finally. "That will do. You may leave us now."

The maid curtseyed and showed herself out the door. Elizabeth turned in her chair to face her husband, but they both waited a few terse seconds after the door clicked behind Alice before either of them spoke.

Darcy rose from his seat on the bed and came to lean on the dressing table beside his wife.

"As pleasant as it is to have you home again, dear, I must ask- What happened to bring you back early? And why is Georgiana so obviously distressed?" Darcy asked.

Elizabeth sighed, now that the telling was actually upon her, and turned to fiddle with the brush laid out on the table.

"I am afraid it is a rather unpleasant story. You remember the young man I wrote you about, Mr. Aldridge?"

Darcy frowned at the name but nodded affirmatively.

"Well, we had thought ourselves rid of him yesterday, since he was supposedly called away on a trip to Town. But that was apparently not the case. Thinking she was rid of his presence, Georgiana was alone in the sitting room when he made a surprise visit." Elizabeth paused in her story as her husband leapt from his stance to angrily pace the room.

"Go on!" he urged her, irritated.

She watched him briefly, unsure if she should, but in the end continued, "When Georgiana rose to summon a chaperone, he apparently produced quite a passionate proposal, which ended when he grabbed her by the arms and attempted to force a kiss upon her."

A growl rose from deep in Darcy's throat, and his hands clenched at his sides.

"Fitzwilliam, calm down," his wife scolded him gently, reaching out to touch his arm. "She punched him, and he was shocked enough to release his grip on her long enough for her to escape to Bingley's study. She's a little jumpy and emotional, but there was no real harm done. Bingley had him removed from the premises and threatened to ruin him if he tried to contact her ever again. Apparently he is quite in the duns."

Darcy stormed away from his wife to look out the window, one fist on the glass. She knew him well enough to grant him the silence he needed to sort through his emotions.

Finally, he sighed and turned back to his wife, drawing a chair nearer to her seat.

"That still does not fully explain her reaction to seeing Crosby again. I would have thought she would be overjoyed upon finding him here," Darcy complained.

"But you forget the circumstances under which they parted," his wife reprimanded him. "Miranda Rycroft had Georgiana convinced that Mr. Crosby was soon to offer for her. She had given up hope that he felt something for her. Then, she has this trying encounter with Mr. Aldridge, combined with an exhausting day of travel, and upon arriving home finds the man she has been trying to forget in the one place she thought she would find peace. It was all just too much."

"Hmmm…" Darcy rubbed his chin. "I see." Although he still did not quite understand what the fuss was about. Women were not always very logical, he reminded himself.

"Do you think she will be ready to face Crosby at dinner?" Darcy asked his wife. "She has only had a few hours to come to grips with his presence here."

Elizabeth beamed at her husband. "I warned her that he was staying to dinner and that she was expected to make an appearance. She has resigned herself. It is enough. All Thaddeus needs is an opportunity. This will all be made right again soon enough."

"I certainly hope so," Darcy muttered. "I don't think I can handle all this drama in my household much longer before I hole myself away in my study like your father."

Elizabeth laughed. "Just wait until your daughter is out in society."

*****

When Thaddeus arrived in the drawing room in which they were to meet before dinner, he found Elizabeth and Darcy waiting on him. Georgiana had yet to make an appearance.

"Good evening Mr. Crosby!" Elizabeth greeted him enthusiastically. "I trust you were able to find sufficient entertainment when my husband abandoned you to attend to me."

"I did indeed," he reassured her. "I have become quite spoiled by having the resources of your vast library at my disposal."

"It is one of the best features of the house," Elizabeth agreed, "and the work of many generations. Darcy is quite proud of it."

"He has reason to be. I have never seen the equal of it," Thaddeus complimented them.

Darcy accepted the compliment with a nod, but remained uncharacteristically silent. Thaddeus couldn't help but wonder what knowledge Mrs. Darcy had imparted to him to have such an effect and wished someone had felt the need to inform him as well.

They all paused in their conversation as the door creaked open and Georgiana entered. She walked regally, her head held high, but Thaddeus could sense the nervousness and embarrassment she was trying to hide.

Elizabeth smiled reassuringly at her, while Darcy could only muster a tight smile. She cocked her head at her brother and lifted one sardonic brow before facing Thaddeus.

She dropped a curtsey as Thaddeus bowed over her hand. With a genuine smile, she said, "Mr. Crosby what a pleasure to find you in Derbyshire. Tell me, what brings you to the area?"

Thaddeus was quite flabbergasted by the smile she had leveled at him and had to take a moment to gather his wits back around him.

Thankfully, the butler arrived at that moment to announce dinner, and Elizabeth took control.

"Perhaps you could tell us over dinner," she suggested. "I too find myself quite curious as to how you found yourself here."

Thaddeus agreed and they turned to go into dinner. He offered his arm to Georgiana. She hesitated briefly, but took it. The warmth of her hand seeped through her glove and his jacket, until he felt distinctly its imprint on his arm. It felt so right to have her on his arm again; she belonged there.

Reacting instinctively, he covered her hand with his own. Her questioning eyes flew to meet his at the gesture. He longed for the opportunity to answer her questions, to restore what was lost between them, but he knew that the time was not yet right. He smiled down at her, giving her unspoken reassurance as he guided her to her seat at the table.

After the first course had been served, Georgiana steered the conversation back to Thaddeus' presence in Derbyshire.

"Are you visiting the Lake District, Mr. Crosby?" Georgiana asked. "It is particularly lush and beautiful this time of year."

Thaddeus glanced at Darcy from the corner of his eye and toyed with his food, unsure how to reveal his true reasons for being there. Darcy avoided eye contact while his wife looked up curiously, waiting for his answer. Apparently he hadn't already told her the news.

"No, I'm not. Although I do hope to be able to tour the area once things settle down some," Thaddeus said. "I'm sure you would be able to recommend some of the local sights."

"I suppose I could do so if you liked," Georgiana said, confusion written on her face.

"I hope to have many opportunities to do so," Thaddeus said, looking up at Georgiana to gage her reaction. "As I've taken up residence in the area."

She still appeared confused. "You've taken up residence? Have Mr. and Mrs. Crosby leased a house in the area?"

"No," Thaddeus said patiently. "I've purchased an estate nearby, Wylington. You are probably familiar with it, as I believe the previous owners were acquainted with you."

Georgiana put down her fork with a clank. "You've purchased Wylington?"

"Yes," Thaddeus said calmly. "Your brother has been kind enough to assist me in my hunt for a new steward."

Georgiana swallowed and said coolly, "I must congratulate you on your acquisition. I am, indeed, acquainted with it. It is a beautiful property. It will make a fine home for your family."

Elizabeth looked up with a start and her gaze flew between the two young people. Thaddeus stared at Georgiana as she returned to her food, her hand shaking as she picked up her fork. What could she mean by that comment?

Surely she must know that he had done it for her, that it was their family he had been thinking of when he purchased it.

But no, the realization slowly dawned on him, she was still under the impression that he meant to marry Miranda! She was picturing Miranda dwelling an easy distance from her, rubbing her conquest in her face. She thought she would have to watch as someone else lived out her dreams.

Thaddeus could not let the moment pass without doing something to relieve her mind. He cast his mind about for a suitable reply

"It is a very pleasant property," he said carefully. "I can only hope that it is far enough away from Town that my sister and her friends will not find it appealing. I had hoped to escape the rigmarole of society, at least for a time."

The statement did not completely have the desired effect, for Georgiana only appeared confused once more by the statement. How he wished for the opportunity to speak openly with her!

He tamped down the frustration that welled within him. The time would come. He must be patient.

The servants came to serve the second course.

"Tell me, Mr. Crosby," Elizabeth said as the servants cleared the plates, "how do you enjoy the country? It is quite a change from Town."

"I find I enjoy it very much," he said with some relief. "The quiet and peace one finds in the country has quite the restorative effect. The people have been very welcoming and friendly. I find myself very pleased with the neighborhood."

"While the company may not be as varied as it is in Town, I think you will find Derbyshire only becomes more agreeable with time," Elizabeth commented.

"I would rather spend my time with a few close friends than have all the variety a ballroom in London can furnish," Thaddeus said wryly.

"I can well understand that," Darcy stated, finally deciding to have a part in the conversation.

The conversation moved in another direction, and Thaddeus was glad to be off the hook, for the moment at least. He was sure Georgiana still had questions for him, but they would have to wait for a more opportune moment. In the meantime, he was glad to be accepted at Pemberley as a neighbor and friend.

After dinner, the ladies left the gentlemen to their port. Elizabeth sent a backwards glance at Darcy as she left the room, which managed to convey her displeasure if the ladies should be left to themselves for too long.

Darcy smiled at his wife's retreating figure and swirled the port in his glass.

"Mark my words, Crosby, in six months time you will see that very look on your own wife's face," Darcy said confidently.

Thaddeus took a sip out of his own glass. "I hope you are right, Darcy. But at the moment I don't have the confidence you do."

Chapter 13

Elizabeth and Georgiana settled into their seats in the drawing room as they waited for the men to join them. Georgiana had picked up some embroidery to work on while Elizabeth held a book unopened on her lap.

"Georgiana," Elizabeth began hesitantly, unsure how to begin this conversation, "I know that the past few months have been very difficult for you and I don't know exactly what happened to change things between you and Mr. Crosby. But I'm pretty sure it has to do with that wretched Miranda Rycroft. I'm not sure what she told you, but whatever it was, she lied. He never had any interest in her. He bought Wylington and moved to Derbyshire for *you*. He was planning to do so long before Miranda even inserted herself into the picture in London. Hear him out."

Georgiana sighed and put aside the embroidery she had abandoned as Elizabeth had launched into her speech.

"I know we need to talk," she admitted. "I just want to find out the truth, and I never will if I don't listen to his side of the story. But it is very difficult to have a private conversation in the midst of a dinner party!"

"Ah! But this is no ordinary dinner party," Elizabeth reminded her. "There is only family present, and Darcy and I will make sure you have the opportunity you need for some private conversation this evening."

She sat back in her chair and picked her book up.

"By the way, I informed your brother of your misadventure yesterday with Mr. Aldridge," Elizabeth slid in slyly.

"You don't think he told Mr. Crosby, do you?" Georgiana cried, mortified at the idea.

"Lower your voice, dear, or the servants will talk," Elizabeth scolded gently. "No, I don't suspect he will. You will have to inform him of the incident yourself when you apologize for your earlier behavior."

Georgiana grumbled under her breath at her sister's directives but did not blatantly disregard them.

"What was that, dear?" Elizabeth asked innocently, knowing exactly what Georgiana's reaction would be.

"Nothing," she muttered petulantly, and picked up her embroidery. She wasn't about to inform Thaddeus of Mr. Aldridge's advances. It was embarrassing enough that the Bingleys and her brother knew, but she would be mortified if Thaddeus ever found out that she had allowed herself to be in such a compromising situation.

The gentlemen joined them soon after. Elizabeth rose and set aside her book.

"Why don't I entertain us with some music?" she suggested. "Fitzwilliam, will you turn the pages for me?"

Darcy's eyes lit up at the prospect of his wife at the pianoforte and he eagerly followed her to the instrument, leaving Thaddeus standing just inside the doorway.

Georgiana glanced up at Thaddeus and smiled shyly. Buoyed by her smile, he approached her and took a seat nearby, close enough that they could talk privately but without crowding her space.

Thaddeus cast about in his mind for some generic topic to start a conversation with. He couldn't just leap right into all the things he really wanted to say.

"I understand, Miss Darcy, that my brother is an uncle again. How is young Geoffrey making the transition from being an only child?" Thaddeus asked.

He seemed to have chosen the right topic, for Georgiana's eyes lit up and her smile broadened as she thought of Geoffrey.

"Not very well, I'm afraid," she admitted, "although he seemed to be coming around more to the idea by the time I left. With the attention a new baby demands, he wasn't getting as much time with his parents as he was used to. But I think, albeit begrudgingly, he is getting rather attached to Eliza. At first he wouldn't come near her, but just yesterday he asked to hold her. He's making good progress, if slowly."

"It sounds like it was a difficult decision to leave early," Thaddeus commented.

"No, not really," Georgiana said softly before swiftly changing the subject. "Do you think Mr. and Mrs. Crosby will visit Chetborn in order to see Eliza before she gets much older?"

"I wouldn't be surprised if they come up to visit once the season has wrapped up and everyone has deserted London for the cooler countryside." He sighed. "Caroline will not be dragged away from 'civilized' society before that, no matter the inducement."

"Really?" Georgiana queried. "I would have thought she would have jumped at the opportunity to inspect your new home and suggest any renovations she felt were needed."

He shook his head. "Our tastes are vastly different. Any renovations can wait until there is a mistress who would like to make it her own." He paused and searched her face, unsure how Georgiana would react to the mention of a mistress.

She looked down at her hands. "I would think that Miss Rycroft's tastes would be very similar to Caroline's."

Thaddeus breathed a sigh of relief; here at last was an opportunity to segue into what he really wanted to talk to her about.

"I'm sure they are," he said, "but I have no intention of allowing her access to my home, especially as its mistress."

"You don't?" Her eyes rose to meet his, and she began tentatively, "But I saw you at the opera together and she informed me of many other occasions where you had been in company together. It certainly seemed that she had hopes in that direction."

"Whatever her expressed hopes were, they were unfounded. She is a member of the same clique Caroline is. Wherever we were invited, the Rycroft's would be also. Caroline tried to push us together, but I was only ever polite to her. Whatever Miss Rycroft said about us was completely fabricated. I avoided her as much as I could. That night at the opera, I was unaware we would be joining the Rycrofts in their box, or I never would have attended," Thaddeus told Georgiana intently, leaning in as he spoke. "Miss Rycroft is manipulative and scheming and she has none of the qualities I desire in a wife."

He took a deep breath, holding back the words that threatened to spill from him at this line of conversation. Now was not the time to make a declaration. It was too soon, he had to give her time. Time to realize that the words he spoke so fervently were true and that his intentions toward her were of the most honorable kind. She needed to know that his feelings were steadfast, and he needed to know that she returned them.

He felt himself drowning in the mesmerizing emerald depths of her eyes and sat back in his seat quickly, breaking the hold she had over him.

He cleared his throat and finished lamely, "Wylington will have to make do without a mistress for the time being."

Georgiana sat back in her chair, as she too had leaned forward in the intensity of their conversation, feeling slightly disappointed by what he hadn't said. She chastised herself, *how can you be expecting a proposal from his lips, when just a few minutes ago you were convinced he was to marry another woman. Am I that fickle in my feelings?*

Thaddeus cast his mind about for a less emotionally charged subject, something that would help them regain their equilibrium.

"Have you had to opportunity to see your niece and nephew since your return?" Thaddeus asked, aware of the regard she held for Thea and Will.

She looked chagrined. "No, I am embarrassed to admit that I haven't visited the nursery yet. I was a little overwhelmed upon my arrival."

Elizabeth, who had been observing the young couple, concluded the lengthy sonata she had been playing and looked up at her husband.

"I believe it is safe to return to the conversation now, dear," she suggested. "Whatever discussion there was to be on sensitive matters is concluded for the night."

They joined Thaddeus and Georgiana just as Thaddeus smiled softly and said, "I am sure they will forgive the oversight. Are they to join us this evening now that dinner has been served?"

"Who are you speaking of?" Elizabeth asked, seating herself beside Georgiana.

"Thea and Will," Georgiana replied. "Are they to be sent down? I admit I neglected to pay them a visit in the nursery."

"I did not want to presume that their presence would be desired among the company tonight," Elizabeth admitted. "But I should very much like to have them down if we are all in agreement. My visit to the nursery was in itself too short for such a lengthy absence."

"I should like that very much," Georgiana approved, and the men both nodded their agreement.

The children were sent for and brought down shortly thereafter. Elizabeth rose to take Will from the nurse's arms. Thea crossed the room very primly and properly before gleefully throwing herself in her aunt's arms.

"Aunt Giana, you *are* back! Mama said you were but I didn't believe it 'cuz you didn't come see me," Thea said, pouting a little by the end of it.

"I'm sorry darling," Georgiana replied. "I wasn't feeling very good when we got home and I had to lie down for a while. I do hope you will forgive me."

"Oh, all right," Thea said impatiently. "Can we play the pianoforte together? I's been practicing for when you came back."

"I don't see why we cannot," Georgiana assured her. "But first, have you made your curtsey to Mr. Crosby? I'm sure you would not wish to appear rude."

The little girl turned and bobbed a quick curtsey to Thaddeus, who said with a grin, "It is a pleasure to see you again, Miss Darcy."

She held her head high regally and sniffed. "Likewise."

The adults in the room hid their smiles as she turned back to Georgiana.

"Now can we play?" she asked.

"Yes, dear," Georgiana acquiesced, taking her by the hand and leading her to the pianoforte.

Elizabeth and Darcy busied themselves with their son, allowing Thaddeus the luxury of observing the interaction between Georgiana and her niece.

He couldn't help but reflect on the woman he loved as he watched her with the people she loved most. She was all the things he remembered her to be. She was quiet, mild, and gentle, with a kind heart and a generous nature. She loved her family fervently and rejected the whims of society. She preferred quiet nights at home to the bustle of the city and she had a passion for music.

And yet, over the last few months he had come to know there was more to her than that. A slight smile quirked the corners of his mouth up. She was also stubborn, strong-willed, and had difficulty trusting men. She was easily embarrassed and quick to think badly of herself.

She was so much more than he had ever dreamed of. Months ago, he had known she was the one, that he would marry her someday. But today, sitting here among those she cared about the most, he could not imagine his life without her. His future held many nights like this one, spent among those he cared about the most. This was his life now. It was here, in the backwoods of Derbyshire, not in some twinkling ballroom, where he had found happiness.

Georgiana felt his gaze upon her and looked up at him to smile gently. He returned her smile, all the love he felt for her shining clearly in his gaze. The intensity of the look in his eyes nearly took her breath away. She could no longer deny what was between them. He was hers, and she was his. There could be no other way. In that moment, all that had stood between them was forgiven and forgotten.

They finished their performance, and the adults clapped enthusiastically as Thea took her curtsey. She beamed at their praise and proudly pranced to her parents' side to regale her mother with stories of what she had missed during the past six weeks. Georgiana sent a glance in Thaddeus' direction before launching into a familiar piece.

As he listened to the notes that had flowed from his own fingers only a few hours ago, a slow smile spread across his face. No music had ever sounded as beautiful to his ears, for no melody had ever been played with the same intent behind it. He listened for a few bars before rising to join her at the instrument, ostensibly to turn the pages once more, although no one there was under the pretense that it was necessary.

Georgiana felt the warmth of his gaze upon her downturned head and the nearness of his presence as he joined her at the pianoforte. Her cheeks flushed hotly at her perceived boldness with the choice of music, but she refused to retreat from her performance. He had to know what this piece symbolized. He had to know that she played it now with one purpose. The notes flowed from her fingers easier than any words ever could. They conveyed her thoughts and feelings with greater clarity than she ever would have been able to express. She only hoped that he could understand the language.

She hazarded a glance upward and the intensity of his gaze nearly took her breath away. There could be no mistaking the depth of feeling in them, and there could be no doubt that he had understood the message she had been trying to send.

In the presence of her family, they could not speak as freely as they wished, but they both knew now that it was only a matter of time. He would declare his intentions soon, and then there would be nothing standing between them and a future together.

*****

The next morning found Georgiana readying for the day with a spring in her step. Her lady's maid found her humming as she went about her toilette. Alice hid her smile as she pulled a morning dress out of the wardrobe. Georgiana paused in brushing her hair to grin at the maid in the mirror.

"It's a beautiful, mornin', miss," Alice greeted the young lady. "It's right pleased I am to see you up and lively this morn."

"It is a lovely day," Georgiana agreed, before frowning slightly at the dress the maid was putting out. "The blue muslin is rather extravagant for a morning spent at home, don't you think?"

"It is a fine dress, miss, for a fine day." Alice busied herself smoothing the wrinkles from the dress. "We wouldn't want Miss to be lookin' anything but your best if any gentleman callers were to come round."

Georgiana blushed at the blatant hint and resumed brushing her hair, offering no further opposition to her maid's choice. Alice fussed with the dress for a few more moments before coming to stand behind her mistress at the dressing table. She took the brush from Georgiana and began to style her hair.

On any ordinary day, Georgiana would have foregone the lengthy process in lieu of a simple hairstyle, but she had high hopes for what this day held. She sat patiently as Alice plaited and curled, teased and tousled, until she had finally coaxed Georgiana's fine locks into an elegant up-do.

Georgiana was pleased with the result. It was not so contrived that she didn't look and feel like herself; but it reflected the elegance and poise she strived for as a gentlewoman.

"It looks beautiful, Alice," Georgiana complimented the maid. "Thank you for your assistance."

The other woman merely nodded in the mirror before turning to help Georgiana into her gown. When they were finished, Georgiana looked the very picture of a modest lady prepared to meet her beau, right down to the twin spots of pink upon her cheeks.

She dismissed the maid and decided to take a few minutes to compose herself before she had to face the rest of her family in the breakfast room. She still had a little time before breakfast would be served, so she sought her journal from its place on the stand beside her bed and pulled a chair up to the window.

The bright rays of sunlight danced upon the paper as she turned to a new, crisp page. She hesitated to mar its brilliance with her thoughts, but the words had been pent up within her too long. It was but a moment before her hand was racing across the page, rushing to express every thought and feeling at once.

For a full ten minutes her hand did not slow, but eventually she concluded, with every emotion spent in the act. Having put her thoughts and feelings in writing, she found herself facing the day with a calm and serenity she had not previously possessed.

With her newfound peace, she found herself quite ready to confront her brother and sister at the breakfast table. She expected to find them waiting for her, but was surprised to find the room empty upon her arrival.

"Have my brother and sister come down to breakfast yet?" she inquired of the butler.

"They have requested breakfast be sent up to their chambers this morning, Miss Darcy," the butler answered formally. "They also requested that I inform you to expect that they will be above stairs until the normal hour for callers. Is there anything further I can assist you with, Miss Darcy?"

"No, thank you," Georgiana murmured, smiling to herself a she moved away to help herself to the buffet laid out on the side table. She should have known that after such an extended separation her brother and sister would be eager for the chance to spend some time alone together.

She filled her plate and poured herself some coffee before settling at the table and picking up the morning paper to savor. She would not have to vie with her brother for the chance to read it this morning.

About the time Georgiana was engrossing herself in the paper, Thaddeus was too sitting down to breakfast. Much simpler fare filled his plate, as he was battling a rather debilitating case of nerves.

Thaddeus sipped gingerly from a steaming cup of black coffee and nibbled on a piece of dry toast. His stomach was tied in knots at the prospect of what he hoped to accomplish today.

His hand slipped to feel for the ring in his pocket, reassuring himself that it was still there, a tangible reminder of the question he had yet to ask and have answered. So many doubts and worries whirled in his mind at what he was about to do.

Was it too early? Should he give her more time? How would she react? What if she didn't like the ring he had chosen for her? Would Darcy give his consent?

His rational mind knew that the time had come, that there was no one else that he would rather spend his life with. He suspected that Georgiana was just as ready and willing as he to enter into the marital state. But his own insecurities were wreaking havoc on his mind.

He withdrew his hand from his pocket with a sigh and resumed attempting to consume some nourishment. He had little appetite for even the modest meal before him, but he knew he needed some sustenance for the day ahead. He lingered over the meal, trying to distract himself by reading the paper, but when he rose from the table it was still far too early to call at Pemberley.

He took himself off to his study, hoping to lose himself in the complexities of the estate ledgers until the time came when he could reasonably present himself at Pemberley.

Several hours later, Thaddeus rose from his desk to stretch his stiff muscles. He crossed to the window and looked out over the lush lawn to the wooded hillside beyond. Wylington might only be a drop in the bucket compared to Pemberley, but he was proud of what he had accomplished there. He knew Georgiana would be too. Together, they would continue to improve on the existing property and house, making it their own in the years to come.

Here they would raise their family, and make memories that would last for a lifetime. He didn't know what exactly the future held for them, but Wylington would be their home. He couldn't wait to share it with her.

He checked the hour on his pocket watch and was pleased to note that he could now set out for Pemberley. He eagerly left his ledgers behind, hastening to be off.

*****

Georgiana too took note of the hour as she ensconced herself in the parlor, anxious for the arrival of a certain expected gentleman. Elizabeth, having finally made an appearance below stairs noted her agitation with amusement. While her sister seemed calm to all outward appearances, and indeed was remarkably so for one waiting expectantly for an admirer to call, her incessant tugging on her embroidery gave away her impatience.

Elizabeth took pity on the younger woman, and sent her off on a pursuit that she knew to be of the utmost advantage in a situation such as this.

"Why don't you go for a walk in the gardens, dear?" she suggested gently.

Georgiana shifted in her seat before admitting, "I would prefer to remain indoors for the time being. I would not wish to be absent if Mr. Crosby were to call."

"There is no need to fear you will miss his visit," Elizabeth reassured. "I am quite capable of keeping him entertained until you can be called in from the gardens. Regardless, I very much doubt that he would leave without seeing you."

Georgiana allowed this to be true, and took herself out to the gardens, making a point not to stray too far from the house itself. Elizabeth was watching her from the window when Darcy joined her in the parlor.

He came up behind her and wrapped his arms around her waist, peering out at his sister over her shoulder.

"I see you've sent Georgiana out to pace," he commented. "Were you concerned for the well-being of the carpets?"

Elizabeth smiled at his teasing and scolded him, "You would make me out to sound like my mother, husband." She paused before continuing, "She is actually rather calm, all things considered. But I thought she was better off waiting with the distraction of nature to engage her. The inactivity of the parlor would only serve to allow her more time to dwell on her nerves."

"You are a wise woman, Mrs. Darcy," her husband commented in her ear, deadpan. "We would not want to encourage her to complain of her "poor nerves" and develop a dependence on smelling salts. Crosby would not thank me for such behavior. It is a far better proposal to allow her nerves some air to breathe and calm themselves."

Elizabeth turned in his arms to swat him mildly on the chest. "For shame, Darcy! You had better hope *I* don't develop a chronic case of the nerves after such a speech as apparently I am genetically predisposed to such adversities."

Darcy held her a little tighter to prevent her from abusing him further, and leaned in to rest his forehead on hers. She relaxed in his arms and smiled at the teasing twinkle in his eyes.

"If I ever begin to lock myself away in the study and disengage socially, I give you full leave to develop a severe case of nerves, my love," Darcy promised.

"You would have more than just my "poor nerves" to contend with if you were ever to attempt such a thing," Elizabeth warned him teasingly.

He smiled down at her. "You may consider me forewarned, madam. I am very well aware that my sister did not learn her left hook from *me*!"

Elizabeth flushed at the insinuation, but did not deny it. There were some things a father of five daughters was concerned about that many would overlook in an upbringing. Her father, while negligent in some areas of their education, and done his duty by them in one sense at least.

"Well," she responded mildly, hoping to brush off her lingering embarrassment at being caught out, "let us just be glad that she knows how to protect herself. Hopefully after today she will have no need to use such knowledge again."

Darcy nodded and opened his mouth to speak, but they were both distracted by the sound of the door opening. Regretfully, they separated as the butler entered to announce their expected visitor.

Both Darcy and Elizabeth smiled upon Thaddeus' entrance into the parlor. He looked around the room and was clearly disappointed not to find Georgiana in attendance.

"Mr. Crosby! What a pleasure to see you again so soon!" Elizabeth greeted him.

Thaddeus was fully aware it was no surprise to anyone in the household that he had returned. He cleared his throat nervously.

"Yes, well, I had hoped to request a private audience with Miss Darcy..." He allowed his sentence to trail off, and Elizabeth took pity on him.

Glancing at Darcy, she said, "Georgiana is in the garden, taking a walk. Perhaps you could find her there?"

Crosby's eye darted to seek Darcy's approval, and he was heartened by the solemn nod he received.

"I shall look forward to receiving you in my study upon your return to the house, Crosby," Darcy said, and Thaddeus smiled at the insinuation of a positive outcome.

"I look forward to it also," he responded. Bowing, he said, "I think I shall take your advice, Mrs. Darcy and find Miss Darcy in the gardens. Thank you for the suggestion." He took his leave of them.

Elizabeth smiled fondly at her husband as he returned to peer anxiously out the window at his sister.

"Perhaps I should have sent you outside to pace," she teased, coming up and wrapping an arm around his waist.

He settled his arm over her shoulders with a sigh and pulled her into his side.

"It seems just yesterday she was Thea's age. It's hard to admit that she is a grown woman, ready to start a life separate from us," he admitted.

"She is a far cry from the girl she was at Ramsgate," Elizabeth said gently. "Mr. Crosby is worthy of her hand."

Her husband sighed. “I know he is. And we are fortunate they are to be settled so nearby at Wylington. We shall see them often. But it is still difficult to let her go.”

“I know, dear,” Elizabeth said with a squeeze. Then Mr. and Mrs. Darcy turned their attention to the scene below them as Thaddeus appeared in the garden.

*****

“Miss Darcy!”

Georgiana looked up with a luminescent smile at the sound of Thaddeus’ voice calling out to her.

“Mr. Crosby,” she greeted him, inclining her head, as he made his way to her side.

“I see you are taking a turn about the gardens,” he said unnecessarily. “May I join you?”

“You may,” she acquiesced, her heart fluttering with expectation.

They walked on companionably, Georgiana pointing out some of the flowers that were her particular favorites as they passed. When they reached a pretty little alcove, with a conveniently located bench, Thaddeus suggested that they sit for a time.

They sat in tense silence for several minutes, Georgiana sneaking glances at Thaddeus as he tried to think of a way to start.

Finally, Thaddeus managed to break the silence. He turned to her, his heart in his eyes and said, “My dear Miss Darcy, I hope you don’t find me too forward in my addresses, but you must allow me to tell you how much

I ardently admire and love you. The periods of separation between us and the misunderstandings that have come between us are naught compared to the depth and sincerity of my feelings for you. I cannot imagine a future without you in it, and having said as much, I would be most deeply honored if you would do me the favor of becoming my wife."

Here he held his breath, awaiting most eagerly her answer. Her eyes shone with unshed tears as she threw her arms around him and made him to understand that her answer was irrevocably in the affirmative. The reader must here forgive the impropriety of such actions, as a declaration such as this must by some necessity involve such open displays affection.

For some time, they sat on the bench, exchanging such assurances of affection and love as those recently betrothed are wont to do. At length, they grew aware of the advancing hour and reluctantly agreed that they must return to the house, he to meet with her brother and obtain his consent; she to inform her sister and receive her congratulations.

They parted with a lingering embrace in the entryway, ignoring the giggling that could be heard coming from behind the parlor door.

Thaddeus found himself knocking on Darcy's study door with some slight trepidation, even though Darcy had encouraged and aided his suit.

He heard Darcy's invitation from within and opened the door to enter. Darcy greeted him with a wry smile that was tinged with sadness and put aside the papers he had been studying.

"I assume that my sister has accepted your offer?" Darcy asked.

"You assume correctly," Thaddeus acknowledged.

"So now all that is left is for me to give my consent," Darcy commented, "although that is hardly necessary since she has reached her majority. You should be glad of that, for I would not be the only one you would have to apply to if it were not so. Colonel Fitzwilliam would not be so easy on you."

"Still, I shall be more at ease, knowing we have your consent," Thaddeus stated.

Darcy sighed and admitted, "You do have it. I could not have parted with her to anyone less worthy of her. It is a comfort to know she will be settled such an easy distance from us."

Thaddeus smiled. "I know that Georgiana finds that comforting as well. She has expressed her satisfaction with remaining so near her family. It is a fact I took very much into consideration as I contemplated my search for an estate."

He sobered before continuing, "You know I shall do my very best, Darcy, to make her happy. I don't have the resources that you have, but I am convinced that love will make up for any deficiencies. She will be well cared for."

"I know," Darcy said. "Georgiana has never been one to prefer the pomp and circumstance that so many of our station find important. In truth, I would wish her to marry for love, no matter the circumstances of the fellow whom she would choose, as I did. I am fortunate that you are able to care for her so well, as it is."

"I'll have my solicitor draw up the marriage contracts for you to look over," Thaddeus commented. "I'd like to procure a special license, if you have no objection. Georgiana and I would prefer to be married here at Pemberley."

"I have no objections," Darcy responded, "and I will have to make arrangements with my banker for Georgiana's dowry to be made available to you once all the paperwork is signed." He smiled. "I am sure my wife and sister will be excited to begin shopping for her trousseau. I suppose a trip to Town will be in order all around."

"Yes, I believe it will be necessary," Thaddeus replied, "but perhaps a few days of rest would be in order first. Your wife and my affianced have only just returned. I am sure they would enjoy some time at home before they begin the wedding preparations."

"You are probably correct," Darcy admitted, frowning. "Is your solicitor in Town? Or have you procured the services of one in Lambton?"

"I thought it better to make the switch to a solicitor in Lambton, since I hope to conduct most of my business from Wylington. I have no desire to be jaunting back and forth from London constantly. Mr. Hawkins was very highly recommended to me by some colleagues of mine," Thaddeus responded.

"Yes, I use him frequently as well," Darcy said approvingly. "He is the best in the area. His services should suffice for your use."

"I am glad to know he has your approval. I shall have him draw up the documents and bring them over for your scrutiny in the next few days or so," Thaddeus said.

"I think that we have covered all the business that is necessary. Shall we adjourn to the parlor and join the ladies? I do hope you shall stay for supper," Darcy invited.

Thaddeus smiled at the much-hoped for invitation. "I shall be delighted to."

Both ladies looked up with a smile at the men's entrance from where they were deep in conversation on the settee. Thaddeus' eyes were immediately drawn to his fiancée. She blushed at his consideration, but her countenance glowed with happiness and a smile could not help but to sneak across her face. Elizabeth gave her sister's hands a squeeze before rising to congratulate her soon-to-be brother-in-law.

She held out her hands to him, pulling him close for a chaste, sisterly kiss on the cheek. "I simply must tell you how pleased I am to be able to call you brother. I am delighted that my beloved sister is to be so happily situated. I do hope we shall have the pleasure of your company for supper?"

Thaddeus' response in the affirmative was met by approval all around, especially in his fiancée's eyes. She joined their little circle by the door, taking Thaddeus' arm as if it was second nature.

The Darcys observed the younger couple's absorption in each other with contentment and shared smiles. The time remaining before supper was filled with happy conversation and joyful laughter all around. It was with great reluctance that the group parted ways to dress for dinner.

Chapter 14

The next few weeks passed pleasantly for all involved. Thaddeus was in attendance at Pemberley almost every day; only the occasional pressing estate business could keep him away for any length of time. Georgiana was quite delighted by this state of affairs and the couple spent much of their time meandering through the gardens, speaking of all that was close to their hearts.

Only one occasion really marked this time period. A few days after the engagement was announced, Thaddeus brought the drawn up marriage contract to Pemberley for approval. He sequestered himself in the study with Darcy to gain that gentleman's support before bringing Georgiana and Elizabeth in to peruse the documents for their approval.

"You have been very generous with her," Darcy commented as he looked over the documents. "You have provided for her far beyond the thirty thousand pounds she will bring to the marriage."

He made a few notations on the paperwork of the sum she was to receive as her dowry.

Thaddeus gulped at the amount the man across from him named so easily.

Darcy looked up sharply at the sound. "Did you not know? I had thought you had taken the amount into consideration when you decided to purchase Wylington."

"No," Thaddeus admitted. "I expected her dowry was likely to be liberal, but I had not thought it to be so vast a sum."

"My father wanted her to be well-taken care of, especially once he realized he would not live to attend to the matter himself," Darcy explained. "There are many who have sought to garner her affection for the sake of her dowry. It is a blessing that she has grown to discern who is a worthy guardian of those funds."

He held up the paperwork. "My father would be very pleased with these settlements."

*****

A week before they were to depart for London to begin preparations for the wedding, Thaddeus decided the time had come for Georgiana to visit Wylington and discuss any remodeling she wished to do. He wanted her to have the opportunity to choose the different fabrics and papers she wished from the greater selections that would be available to them while they were in Town.

Georgiana allowed herself to be handed out from the carriage with a mixture of excitement and trepidation. She was excited for the opportunities that were now open to her as the soon to be mistress, but she was afraid of how her ideas for improvement would be met.

Her brother and sister alighted behind her, along as chaperones for the tour. Thaddeus greeted them all warmly, eagerly offering Georgiana his arm as he turned to introduce her to the staff.

Most of the staff members were familiar to Georgiana, as she had been a frequent visitor of the Brightmore daughters. Even among those she had not had reason to interact with before were many that were known to her. In such an intertwined community as Lambton, many of those who served at Wylington were related to those who served her own family.

The members of the staff were delighted to have such a well-liked young lady for their new mistress. They had all heard such agreeable accounts of her to ensure their approval of the new master's choice of bride.

Georgiana inclined her head and endeavored to remember the name of each one introduced to her. She drew on connections where she could find them and listened intently where there were none. In all, she painted such a charming picture that there was nary a soul who would dare to say anything against the new mistress.

Elizabeth and Darcy stood a distance away, observing their interaction with the servants.

"She is a far cry from the girl you introduced me to in Lambton," Elizabeth murmured to her husband. "See how she glows with confidence. There is no stuttering or stumbling over her words. They are all half in love with her already."

"Yes," her husband said with just a hint of wistfulness in his gaze. "None would dare call her proud now. She has charmed them all. Her manners are just what a lady's ought to be. She has you to thank for that, my dear; under your tutelage she has blossomed into a gentlewoman."

His wife smiled at the praise. "We need have no fear of her competence now. Surely, Fitzwilliam, you can see that she is ready for this step."

"I know she is," Darcy admitted, "but I can't help wishing I never had to let her go anyway." He sighed and patted his wife's hand. "If it is so hard to give my sister her independence, I can't imagine the difficulty when it is time for Thea to marry."

She laughed lightly. "Well, darling, at least you have many years to come to terms with that inevitability."

Thaddeus and Georgiana returned to their relatives, and all four proceeded inside to tour the house. There was very little that Georgiana wanted to change in the public rooms, as the former mistress' taste was to her liking. But it was obvious when they entered the family's quarters that the money had been spent on redecorating the rooms visitors would see.

The upstairs sitting room, music room, and bedrooms were all out-dated. The furniture was worn, and the curtains threadbare. The one bright spot in the music room was a brand new pianoforte that had been sent up from London just that week.

Much time was spent in Georgiana's exclamations of delight over the instrument and inspection of its parts. She sat down eagerly and played a short ditty on it before she reluctantly allowed herself to be drawn away to inspect the master's and mistress' chambers, which were last on the tour.

Darcy and Elizabeth chose to loiter behind as they reached these rooms, allowing the engaged couple some privacy to discuss these most intimate chambers.

Thaddeus had some idea of the changes that Georgiana would wish to make in the suite. The woven materials in the room were sadly tattered and the wallpaper had long since faded into a dingy gray. But he hoped she would see the potential that he saw in the spacious rooms. This was to be their sanctuary from the world, their own private refuge where they could find comfort and companionship in one another's arms.

He took her first into the sitting room that connected the two chambers and allowed her to explore. She walked around the room, dragging her fingers along the backs of the chairs and checking the view from each window. She noted pleasurably a little writing desk he had found in the attics and had set up by one of the windows. She tried out the window seat, perching daintily on its edge, although he knew she longed to curl up on it as he had often found her in Chetborn's library.

Finally she grew curious to look beyond the room and went to one of the connecting doors, peering over her shoulder impishly at Thaddeus before opening the door.

She peeked in and blushed prettily when she realized she had stumbled into the master's chambers. She cast a shy glance at Thaddeus, and boldly stepped into the room to explore further.

Thaddeus only trusted himself to follow her as far as the doorway. He leaned against the doorframe as she delved farther into the masculine rooms. His dressing room lay beyond the bedroom, but that held little appeal for her and she left it after only a cursory glance. The bedroom was fraught with heavy, dark furnishings that stood in stark contrast to her dainty form as she paused next to them.

Georgiana was surprised to have this glimpse into Thaddeus' privacy and could not help but note some of his personal effects that littered the room. He had obviously put some effort into making to room presentable, ostensibly for her viewing pleasure. But there were still things that marked it as his and allowed her the chance at a peek into his life that she would not otherwise enjoy.

A book sat on the bedside table, half read. She gently touched the bowl and pitcher that sat on a stand for his use in the morning, and the razor lying on a towel to dry. She hazarded a glance at her fiancé and found him studying her with such a longing in his eye that she immediately had to turn away, ostensibly to peruse farther.

The heavy furniture was not to her taste, but it suited the room and the man who inhabited it, so she could find no reason to change it. Finally, she had explored the room to her fill. There would be further opportunities for her to become more intimately acquainted with the master's quarters.

She moved on to what would become her chambers, passing by Thaddeus to do so. Thaddeus followed her to the mistress' chambers, eager to see her reaction to the room. Georgiana was far more thorough in her investigation here. She could see that Thaddeus had put some effort into furnishing the room in a way that would appeal to her.

The furniture here was light and feminine, with more decorative detail. He had avoided making any changes to the color scheme, knowing she would probably prefer to make those choices herself. The room lacked any personal effects, but she could see the potential it held. There were large windows looking out over the garden. The light from the windows bathed the room in warmth. It would be a very pleasant place to spend the morning in. There was space for a large fire to be lit in the grate and the room wasn't plagued by the draughts that often made rooms uncomfortable.

She moved on to the dressing room and was pleased with the space and layout. The wardrobes were large and spacious, with plenty of room for her gowns and undergarments.

Over all, she was very pleased with the accommodations. If the space was a little smaller than her current living arrangements, she found them all the most satisfying for their coziness and warmth. All that was needed before she was to inhabit it, besides a little remodeling, was some of her own personal effects to make it home.

She returned to the doorway, where Thaddeus was waiting for her. Seeing him standing, one shoulder against the door frame, watching her lovingly, suddenly brought home to her that her future held many nights with her husband at her door. She blushed at the thought but couldn't help the small smile that escaped her.

Thaddeus met her eyes with a knowing smile, but didn't comment on the thoughts reflected on her face.

"Do you find the rooms satisfactory, Georgiana?" he asked instead. She flushed with pleasure at his use of her first name.

"Yes, very much so," she responded. "I think I shall be quite content."

"Are there many changes you wish to make?" he queried.

"Not so many as you might suppose," she replied, taking his arm as they turned back to join the others. "I should like to change the paper and update the draperies. New linens for the beds are probably in order, and the rugs will need replacing. But I believe the furniture will do quite nicely, with the exception of one or two pieces that are in dreadful need of new upholstery. Do you agree?"

"I do," he agreed. "I had suspected as much upon my initial review of the suite. Shall you be able to make your selections while we are in Town? I should like to begin the renovations as soon as possible so they may be completed before the wedding takes place."

"I believe so," she said with a laugh. "There should be enough time between dress fittings for me to peruse the samples!"

They painted a pretty picture as they returned to where Elizabeth and Darcy awaited them. Their heads were bent together as they walked, talking animatedly and laughing gaily. His unruly, dark head was a studied contrast to her pretty, blonde locks, but Elizabeth and Darcy couldn't help but reflect on how well-suited for one another the pair was.

The couples toured the grounds and enjoyed their afternoon tea before the time came for the Darcys to depart. Thaddeus handed Georgiana into the carriage with a promise that he would be at Pemberley for supper, and as the carriage drove off, all involved were quite satisfied with the day's outcome.

*****

From that day on, time flew more quickly than even the previous weeks had passed. So much was to be accomplished before the eventual nuptials that neither saw as much of the other as they wished. The few weeks spent in Town were sufficient for the acquisition of the trousseau and the materials for Wylington. The business matters necessary took far less time than these pursuits, and long before they departed for Pemberley every 't' was crossed and 'i' dotted.

Thaddeus was obliged to depart London for Wylington to begin construction before Georgiana had completed her shopping. The separation was painful to all involved, as Georgiana's sighs were wont to grate on her brother's nerves and even Elizabeth found herself wishing for the wedding to be done and over with so peace would return to her household.

Once the family was again safely ensconced at Pemberley, the young couple were able to meander through the gardens once more and talk of all that delighted them. But even this time was greatly limited by the necessity of Thaddeus' oversight of his projects at Wylington, and thus it was with great expectation that the day of the wedding arrived.

The ceremony was simple and the bride resplendent in blue. The groom, as nervous and eager as every gentleman in that position is likely to be, stumbled his way through his vows as his bride smiled encouragement. When at last they were pronounced man and wife, many in attendance could be seen raising their handkerchiefs to wipe discreetly at teary eyes. Even Caroline Crosby was not unaffected. If she rejoiced over the acquisition of Miss Darcy as a sister-in-law after all, or over the beauty of the ceremony, cannot be said. But tears of joy were shed.

Afterwards, at the wedding banquet, Mrs. Darcy could be heard remarking to Mr. Darcy on the radiance and confidence displayed by the new Mrs. Crosby. Indeed, all there were astonished by the transformation Georgiana had undergone. Shy and hesitant no more, with her husband at her side, she glowed with enthusiasm and joy in her new situation in life.

Congratulations having been given, and a good time had by all, the bride and groom were at last seen off to their new home at Wylington.

Mr. and Mrs. Crosby retired to the music room soon after their arrival, as Mrs. Crosby was most eager to try out the instrument, and Mr. Crosby was most eager to please his new wife.

Thaddeus repaired to a nearby chair in order to observe Georgiana from the most auspicious angle. She seated herself at the instrument and began to play with almost child-like delight. As she settled into the music, gradually her performance grew more passionate, the notes resounding through the house.

Thaddeus could not help but be enthralled by her playing, knowing that he was observing her at her most unguarded. Here was a side of her that only he was privileged to see.

As gradually as the music had reached its crescendo, she progressively brought the piece back down to its close.

Once the last notes had died down, she met his eyes across the instrument.

"You asked me once if I ever played duets, Mr. Crosby. Are you not going to renew the request?" she asked shyly.

Thaddeus smiled at the hint. "I should very much like to renew the request, Georgiana, but you must learn to call me Thaddeus now that we are married. Mr. Crosby has always brought to mind my brother, not me."

"Very well… Thaddeus." She blushed as she said his name.

His smile broadened, and he got up to join her at the instrument. Once he was seated beside her, their arms brushing, he asked, "What do you wish to play, my dear? Remember I am not so accomplished as you."

She developed a teasing glint in her eye. "I know very well you are more accomplished than you pretend to be. But I shall allow that you may need the music for the piece I should like to play."

"What piece is that?" he asked, having some knowledge of what she desired.

"I think you shall recognize it if you hear it," she said slyly, and played a few bars.

He smiled as his suspicions were confirmed. "You are quite correct. I know that piece very well and you are fortunate that I do indeed have the music."

He shuffled through the sheets set before them until he found the one he was looking for. Together they played the music that had brought them together to begin with.

As the music drew to a close, Thaddeus turned to Georgiana and asked, "How did you know I was able to play this piece?"

"I heard you, that first night back at Pemberley," she said softly. "It is what convinced me that you still truly did care for me. You played so earnestly, I could not help but feel that it was for me."

"It was for you," he admitted. "You would not let me close enough to express how I was feeling and clear up the misunderstandings between us. The only way I could reach you was through music. But even then, I never believed that you would hear me."

"I heard you," she said, her sincerity drawing him closer. "It was *our* song. I dared to hope that there was only one reason for you to be playing it."

He smiled down at her teasingly. "I am glad to know that all of our misunderstandings can be cleared up so easily."

And then he closed the inches that separated them to press a lingering kiss to her willing lips.

Epilogue

There is neither time nor space to recount all that has passed since that day. Suffice it to say that Georgiana and Thaddeus were assured of every happiness in life. The halls of Wylington were filled with laughter and music. In time, children's voices were added to the mix, and many an evening found Mr. and Mrs. Crosby and their children ensconced in the music room, playing and singing while a cheery fire crackled in the background.

The young couple had their differences, as any couple does, but they always managed to put their misunderstandings behind them at the pianoforte. If it was unusual for a gentleman to be found at the keys, it was not remarked upon by anyone in the household.

With the Darcy's they were always on the most intimate of terms. Thaddeus, as well as Georgiana, really loved them; and they were both ever sensible of the warmest gratitude towards the persons who, by bringing her to Chetborn, had been the means of uniting them.

Don't miss the next book by Lelia M. Silver!
Coming November 2012

An Unexpected Lady

Chapter 1

What an inauspicious beginning, Kitty Bennet mused as blood-curdling wails rent the air of the humble parsonage in Kent. Young William Collins had not ceased crying since the moment he had come into the world. Now, two weeks later, poor Charlotte looked positively bedraggled, and the rest of them were hardly faring any better. The only one who seemed at all well-rested was Mr. Collins, which Kitty suspected was in large part due to his ability to escape the parsonage under the guise of attending to church duties. More than once, she had been sent to fetch Mr. Collins from the church, only to find him asleep on the pew. If she had known what awaited her, she would have been sorely tempted to refuse Charlotte's request that she attend her during her confinement.

She gazed longingly out the window at the inviting gardens and warm spring sunshine. Two years ago, she would not have hesitated to abandon Charlotte for the fun of the outdoors. But time spent in her sisters' good company, without Lydia's bad influence, had changed her. She felt the weight of responsibility all too clearly now of the role she had assumed by agreeing to attend Charlotte.

A sudden silence caused hope to flutter briefly in her breast. *Silence, blessed silence!* Kitty never thought to be so grateful for the hush. Her temples throbbed from the constant caterwauling, and lack of sleep had only amplified her headache. The pins that held her mass of curls in a neat chignon were like needles jabbing her scalp.

From above stairs, the wailing started up again. She flinched at the obnoxious sound. She could stand the pressure on her head no more. She tore the pins from her hair, allowing it to cascade around her shoulders. The relief was instant, and she hurried upstairs to put the pins away on her dressing table and find the nurse.

She found the haggard woman in the nursery, cradling the child against her and bouncing him as she paced by the windows.

"Let me take him," she offered. "Wrap him up well and I'll take him out to the gardens. The spring air and sunshine will be good for him."

The grateful woman hastened to do as she asked. Within ten minutes, Kitty found herself in her own spencer, cradling the baby as she walked the garden path. Her bonnet lay rejected inside in deference to the pounding headache that still held her captive.

The combination of the fresh air and warmth from the sun's rays seemed to work miracles on the little boy. Fifteen minutes of walking had calmed him and very nearly put him to sleep. His little body had relaxed into hers and Kitty was murmuring soft nonsense to him when a commotion up the drive drew her attention. Two riders were approaching the parsonage.

She changed her direction to meet them at the gate, not wanting the visitors to disrupt the household while they were finally enjoying a well-deserved respite.

As they drew nearer, Kitty recognized Colonel Fitzwilliam, but the identity of the second rider continued to elude her. He wore his hat low over his face, preventing her from getting a good look at his features.

"Good morning!" Colonel Fitzwilliam called out, drawing his mount close to the garden gate. He dismounted to approach her, throwing the reins of his mount to his companion to hold.

"I trust your morning has been pleasant, Miss Bennet," he said agreeably.

She acquiesced, holding her voice to low tones in order to prevent waking the babe. She wondered that he did not introduce his friend; but there were many in the Fitzwilliams' circle of friends that would consider her beneath their notice.

"I have come with instructions to invite the household to dinner. My wife and her mother desire the company of your party this evening."

"I shall inform Mr. Collins, sir." Normally outgoing, Kitty dreaded the idea of being in company that evening. But the obsequious Mr. Collins would never refuse an invitation from his beloved patroness. She would be obliged to attend.

"Very good then."

His companion's horse whinnied loudly as Colonel Fitzwilliam's mount strayed too close to it.

Kitty's startled gaze rose to meet the stranger's blue eyes as he studied her intently from under the brim of his hat. For one long moment, Kitty could not look away from him, lost in the intensity of his gaze. Then young William let out a earsplitting wail of complaint at being woken so rudely. Immediately, her attention shifted to the baby she held, and the Colonel bid her a hasty adieu, mounting his horse and trotting rapidly down the lane.

The stranger watched her unnoticed as she headed back down the path towards the house, cooing to the baby and bouncing him, before turning his mount to follow his friend.

*****

Nathaniel Watson was not a man who tolerated idiocy. He ground his teeth in an effort to control himself as Lady Catherine began another of her long-winded discourses. When he had accepted Colonel Fitzwilliam's offer to visit him and his new bride, he had not expected to have the mother-in-law in constant attendance also. One would think the woman would accept that her rightful place was in the dowager house!

The occupants of the drawing room seemed to accept her presence as matter-of-course. He desperately needed a distraction, but their dinner guests were not expected to arrive for a half hour yet. He allowed his mind to wander to the expected guests.

He had jumped at the chance to accompany Fitzwilliam to the parsonage in order to extend the invitation. The fresh air had whisked away the vestiges of the dank drawing room and invigorated him. Even his high-spirited mount seemed pleased to have escaped the confines of his stall, surging and shying at any movement, eager for a good run.

They had approached the gates of the parsonage all too soon. Enthralled with the joy of the ride, he did not notice the woman who came to meet them until they were practically upon her. She studied him curiously as he took Fitzwilliam's reins, but appeared to dismiss his presence as his companion began to speak.

He had frowned as he studied her. Her dress marked her as genteel, but her hair was loose, cascading around her shoulders in lush, satin waves. She did not wear a bonnet, in utter disregard for the bounds of propriety. And she did not even appear embarrassed to be caught so!

Still, something about her intrigued him. Her features were dainty and feminine, pretty- but nothing extraordinary. A small part of him admired her audacity to appear so carefree in public, and he couldn't deny that he found her attractive with her tresses flowing free. Still, there was nothing at all about her that would set her apart from the masses of debutantes seeking a title and a fortune.

In his distraction, he had neglected to pay attention to his high-strung mount. Colonel Fitzwilliam's gentle roan ambled too close to his own gelding, and his mount struck out at the other horse, whinnying loudly in protest.

The young woman's eyes had snapped up at the interruption. Instantly, he was drowning in her clear, bottle green gaze. Her eyes held a hint of irritation, but any other discoveries he might have made were lost when a baby's cry split the air. His eyes had been drawn downward to a bundle she had been cradling that he had hitherto ignored.

He had been startled to realize the bundle she held was actually a child. What was she doing with a baby? She certainly did not seem to be old enough for the child to be hers.

Colonel Fitzwilliam had come scurrying back to collect his mount as the cries grew in intensity. Nathaniel had watched the woman as she hurried away. He still couldn't explain why the idea of the child being hers bothered him so much.

He noted with pleasure that the time had neared for their guests to arrive. Surely now some of his questions would be answered.

As if on cue, the door opened to admit their guests.

"A Mr. William Collins, Miss Maria Lucas, and Miss Catherine Bennet," the footman intoned drolly.

Nathaniel studied the additions to their party as introductions were made. He was inexplicably disappointed to see that the young lady he had admired earlier had been restored to her proper dress. She wore a simple, yet elegant, gown and her hair was curled and piled on top of her head in the latest fashion. He saw none of the free spirit that had so enthralled him earlier. In their place was a dull, subdued girl that he easily dismissed as unimportant.

*****

Kitty barely paid any heed as the introductions were made. Her mother would have been horrified to note with what little enthusiasm she shared the room with the decidedly single Marquess of Rockingham. Her head pounded fiercely from the myriads of pins that pressed against her scalp, holding up her mass of hair. In her exhaustion, every movement was excruciating, and when she moved it felt as if her limbs were weighted down with stones.

She took a seat next to Maria Lucas on the settee and tried to maintain an attentive air as Mr. Collins greeted his patroness with excessive admiration. Lady

Catherine monopolized the conversation, her sharp, intrusive voice pausing only for Mr. Collins' flattery.

It was with some relief that the entire party went in to dine. Kitty found herself seated, in a surprising move, to Lady Catherine's left, with the Marquess seated across from her and Mr. Collins to her left. She tried not to allow the shock to show on her face as she took her seat.

It soon appeared that Lady Catherine had engineered such a situation for a purpose. As sister of the despised Elizabeth Darcy, who had upset her long hoped for plans, Lady Catherine was intent on exposing all her deficiencies for the table at large.

"How is your sister, Miss Bennet?" Lady Catherine asked with a smirk. "I hope she is not finding the rigors of Town too challenging."

"You will have to be more specific as to which sister you are referring to," Kitty replied. "I have four, as you are aware."

Lady Catherine sniffed irritably. "I was referring to Miss Elizabeth. She is the only one of your sisters I am acquainted personally with, although I am aware of your youngest sister and that patched-up marriage of hers."

Kitty blushed at the insinuation, but ignored the jab and responded mildly, "My sister Elizabeth is enjoying the opportunity to sample the pleasures of Town. There is a stubbornness about her that never can bear to be frightened at the will of others. Her courage rises with every attempt to intimidate her. The trait has only grown since she has become Mrs. Darcy."

Lady Catherine frowned at the mention of Elizabeth's married name. "She always did give her opinion very decidedly for so young a person. I am sure my nephew will tire of that soon enough. He will turn to those befitting his station before long."

Kitty lifted her chin. "You will have to excuse me for choosing to believe otherwise. It would hardly encourage sisterly affection if I did not wish the best for my sister in her marriage."

The lady harrumphed and momentarily applied herself to her meal, allowing Kitty to sigh in relief and attend to her own plate. But the reprieve was only momentary, and soon Lady Catherine was on the attack again.

"I hope that you have applied yourself to become accomplished in the areas which your sister neglected. No excellence in music, or any other pursuit, is to be acquired without constant practice. I have told *Miss Bennet* this several times, that she will never play really well unless she practices more."

Kitty raised a brow at Lady Catherine's use of her sister's maiden name. "I believe Mr. Darcy finds Mrs. Darcy's playing to be quite satisfactory. Exquisite even. I fear I cannot say the same about my own. My sister Mary is said to be quite accomplished at the pianoforte, but I never showed any affinity for the instrument."

"Do you draw then?"

"Not at all."

"I never heard of such a thing!" She turned and applied to the Marquess for the first time in the conversation. "Lord Rockingham, surely you have never heard of such a deficiency in a young lady's education among your circles."

He met Kitty's eyes over the table, his expression indecipherable. "No. I have not."

Kitty lowered her eyes to her plate. She was beginning to tire of this line of inquiry. An attack on her person was not what she had had in mind for the evening's entertainment, especially in her current state. She had endeavored to address Lady Catherine with every appearance of civility, even when that lady had not shown her the same consideration.

Fortunately, Lady Catherine believed her point to be made from Lord Rockingham's reply and left off interrogating Kitty in favor of expounding upon her own many virtues. Mr. Collins was eager to support her in this line of discussion and he inserted his own praises on the subject with delighted alacrity.

Kitty could not help but feel her own inferiority at that moment, and lacking the courage that her sister possessed, applied herself to her dinner without an upward glance.

*****

Nathaniel looked forward to the separating of the sexes after dinner with some trepidation. Had Colonel Fitzwilliam been the only other gentleman present, he would have looked to the occasion with pleasure, but the presence of the parson complicated matters. He had the uneasy feeling that he would become the focus of the man's obsequious manners in Lady Catherine's absence.

He was right to be so concerned, for upon the ladies' removal to the drawing room, Mr. Collins shifted his attention to his prestigious person with such flattery and groveling that Nathaniel began to suspect that the parson had put much forethought into arranging his elegant compliments. Colonel Fitzwilliam watched it all with a glint of laughter in his eye.

At length, Nathaniel could stand it no longer, and his suggestion that they join the ladies in the drawing room was met with approval.

They entered the room to find Lady Catherine holding court over the ladies. There was nothing beneath that lady's attention when it could furnish her with an occasion of dictating to others. He noted that Miss Bennet was again the object of Lady Catherine's attention and he could not help but pity the young woman her fate.

He purposefully took a seat as far away from the great lady as possible. Colonel Fitzwilliam joined him on the outskirts of the group, while Mr. Collins eagerly sought out a seat beside his patroness in order to further ingratiate himself.

The two gentlemen began to speak in low tones as Lady Catherine lectured.

"Well, Fitzwilliam, how has marriage been treating you? I do not envy you your new relations."

"Ah, but you forget that they are not new. I have been attending my aunt for many years now." He smiled indulgently at the thought of his new bride. "I find I am quite enjoying married life. Anne is very accommodating and she makes very few demands on my time. We are content to be in each other's company."

"You claim to feel some affection for her, yet you allow her mother to usurp her rightful place in the household. I confess that I am confused by your actions."

"Anne has no desire for confrontation. My father has offered us one of his estates in the North. We will withdraw there shortly, allowing Lady Catherine to live out her days at Rosings. She could not be happy without some employment to occupy her. Here, she can be most active among the cottagers, sallying forth to settle their differences, silence their complaints, and scold them into harmony and plenty. Our absence will hardly be noted. But *hers* will be most appreciated in our new home."

Here, Kitty was dispatched across the room to display her limited skills at the pianoforte for the company. Nathaniel suspected it was an attempt on Lady Catherine's part to embarrass the young woman further, for she had specifically noted over dinner that she had no affinity for the instrument.

As she began to hesitantly pick out a simple tune, Colonel Fitzwilliam said slyly, "Are you still as confirmed a bachelor as ever? I thought perhaps some young lady had caught your eye earlier. Miss Bennet is thought to be uncommonly pretty."

Nathaniel turned his head to observe her lazily at the instrument before declaring, "Yes, but so are half the daughters of the Ton. There is nothing extraordinary enough about her to tempt me."

Kitty faltered at that moment in her playing, her color high, and he thought for a moment that she had overheard their conversation. But he soon dismissed the notion, in favor of the thought that her concentration would by necessity have been fully upon the instrument and not upon themselves. The blush upon her cheeks was easily explained away as embarrassment over the faulty notes.

He gave no more thought to the matter, instead turning the discussion to more agreeable topics.

*****

It was indeed embarrassment that brought color to Kitty's cheeks, but it was not due to her faulty playing. She knew herself to be unequal to the task of performing, and so had no false hopes that she would be able to complete her tenure at the instrument without mistakes.

Her blush was due to the comments of a certain gentleman, which although not loud enough to carry to those gathered on the other side of the room, were quite loud enough to be overheard by her.

Kitty parted from the company that night feeling very small indeed. She had known herself to lack the wit and vivacity of Elizabeth and to be inferior in beauty to Jane. She had not the knowledge of Mary, neither her ability to play and sing, nor did she possess Lydia's high spirits. But it was the first time she had ever felt herself to be positively *ordinary*. She had nothing to recommend her beyond her newly acquired family connections from sisters' recent marriages.

She wished at that moment for the comfort of her sisters' arms. She remembered many a time in their youth when they had crowded five to a bed when one or the other of them had suffered some slight or set-back. How she longed for someone to confide in, to ease her wounded spirit!

But she had only a pillow to entrust her tears to, and an empty room to hear her sorrows.

Chapter 2

The next morning dawned bright and cheerful, and with it it brought a desire to escape that dreadful house. For the moment, young William Collins slept on, and Kitty felt justified in setting off for a short walk in the park in order to sort her feelings from the night before.

Her headache from the day prior had subsided enough that she was comfortable wearing her bonnet, even with her hair in a simple up-do.

She set off down one of the less traveled lanes of the park, hoping for some privacy. It was not to be. She had only traversed a short distance when a rider approached her from behind. She moved to the side of the lane to allow the rider to pass.

Instead, the clip-clop of the horse's hooves slowed and drew abreast of her. Curious and a little confused, she turned to observe her companion as he reined in beside her.

Her attention was so immediately caught by the superior example of horseflesh before her that she neglected to detect the identity of its rider. A chuckle from above finally drew her attention.

"I am glad to see that Abaccus has met with your approval, Miss Bennet," Nathaniel said with a warm smile.

"He moves beautifully," she agreed, casting her eye once more over the tall bay.

"Yes, he has a very smooth gait. A touch too high-spirited, but I would not have a mount any other way."

"He must be great fun to ride," Kitty said enviously.

He tilted his head curiously to study her, recognizing the jealous tone in her voice. "Do you enjoy riding, Miss Bennet?"

"I do," she admitted. "But I do not often have the opportunity. The horses on my father's estate are mostly for use around the farm."

He raised an eyebrow sardonically. "A farm horse is a very different animal than a Thoroughbred like Abaccus. I think you would find him to be more than you can handle."

She frowned at his condescending manner and replied, "I am sure many would agree with you. If you will excuse me now, I'd like to continue my walk." She turned and resumed walking.

Nathaniel scowled at her retreating form and swung out of the saddle to follow. He easily caught up to her in a few long strides.

"May I join you?" he asked.

Her bonnet hid her glower. "If you would like," she said politely, her voice cool. She picked up the pace, which he easily matched.

"Have I said something to offend you, Miss Bennet?" he asked at the decidedly frosty silence that stretched between them.

"Whatever would give you that idea?" she replied sarcastically.

Nathaniel was taken aback. His mouth hung open for a moment before he snapped it shut, stunned into silence. In all his twenty-seven years, no woman had ever spoken to him so!

He had encountered simpering misses, who agreed with every word that came out of his mouth, and accomplished flirts who enticed and teased with every utterance. But no woman had ever treated him with such disregard. If he did not know better, he would think that she did not wish for the privilege of his company!

He puzzled over how to respond to her comment. "Miss Bennet, if you truly do not wish for my company, I assure you that you may say so freely."

She turned her head to look at him, still walking furiously. "I– " Her foot caught on a root in that instant and she went stumbling forward.

There was no time for thought, only for action. Nathaniel, every bit the gentleman he had been raised to be, immediately stepped before her to prevent her from tumbling to the ground.

She fell into his arms with a cry. He grunted as her full weight hit his chest and closed his arms around her to steady her.

"Are you all right Miss Bennet?" he asked solicitously.

She raised her head to meet his eyes, her cheeks flushed with embarrassment. "I believe so, Lord Rockingham. I am dreadfully sorry."

With the immediate danger past, Nathaniel could not help but notice how delicate her petite frame felt in his arms. Her eyes were a deeper shade of green today, he realized, and in their depths he could see chagrin and a lingering trace of hurt. He wondered at that hurt and was opening his mouth to speak when a cry from down the lane drew both of their attentions.

"MISS BENNET!" Mr. Collins stood at the end of the lane, where it intersected with the main path, his mouth agape.

Nathaniel was suddenly aware that he still held Miss Bennet in his arms, most inappropriately. He released her immediately, a sinking feeling in his gut appearing as he realized how their stance would have looked to the parson.

Kitty hurriedly took several steps away from Lord Rockingham, confused by the sudden bereavement she felt as Nathaniel let her go.

Mr. Collins advanced down the lane toward them, his short legs carrying him as fast as they would go. Despite the gravity of the moment, the absurdity of his movements elicited a strangled giggle from Kitty. Nathaniel turned to look down at her dancing eyes and could not help but grin in return.

He sobered quickly as the diminutive man stopped in front of Miss Bennet and drew himself up to his full height. "I am ashamed, Miss Bennet, to call you my cousin! I had thought you to be an upright woman, bound by propriety. But I find instead that I have been harboring a harlot!"

Kitty gasped at the strong words, and Nathaniel felt his own ire rising at the pompous fool.

Mr. Collins continued, "You are no better than that scandalous sister of yours, trying to seduce a member of the Quality! You will return to the house at once and pack your belongings! I will not have a temptress in my household, influencing my wife and child! When I complete my business with Lady Catherine, I will expect you to be ready to depart for the stagecoach immediately!"

Nathaniel watched in horror as the young woman bowed her head and hurried off in the direction of the parsonage, her cheeks burning with embarrassment and rage at the undeserved disparagement.

Nathaniel braced himself for a similar barrage to be heaped upon himself as Mr. Collins turned to him. Instead, he stood in shock as the man proceeded to heap apologies upon him for Miss Bennet's supposed advances. He was repeatedly assured that the young woman would be dealt with properly and that there would be no damage to his own reputation.

His mouth settled in a grim line as he listened to the man. Was Miss Bennet to hold all the blame for the compromising encounter, with no opportunity for explanation? And was he to be completely absolved of all responsibility, simply because of his status as a peer of the realm?

The discrepancy was too great, even for his privileged mind. Troubled, he cut off Mr. Collins. "I have some matters of business to attend to, Mr. Collins, and I believe you have a meeting with Lady Catherine. I recommend that you appear punctually, as that great lady does not like to be kept waiting. Please excuse me."

He turned his back and walked away, leaving the little man to bluster and sputter his compliments incoherently. He had some matters to discuss with Colonel Fitzwilliam.

*****

Kitty's cheeks burned with embarrassment and righteous indignation as she began the process of packing her trunk. Charlotte had offered her the help of one of the maids, but she preferred to complete the task herself.

Insufferable man! The audacity! To accuse her of such filthy things, without even asking for an explanation when he stumbled upon them! It was not as if they had done anything wrong. She had stumbled, and Lord Rockingham had caught her. There was nothing improper in that. It was all a simple misunderstanding.

But she knew that in Mr. Collins' eyes, she was already ruined. It mattered not what the real story was. He had jumped to conclusions and condemned her. The tale would spread. Mr. Collins was incapable of keeping any tidbit of gossip to himself. Lady Catherine was undoubtedly already aware of her disgrace.

That lady would do her best to spread the gossip, to ensure her humiliation in all the best society. Her hatred for Lizzy had already shown itself to extend to her relations. She was to be sent home in shame.

As for Lord Rockingham- she banged the lid of the trunk down angrily- that man would suffer no ills from the occasion. Only *her* reputation would be damaged. Compromised, that was what she was now. Damaged goods. No one would want her.

She knew him better than to think he would offer for her. He was too far above her. Why should he- a *Marquess*- align himself with her, a little nobody from Hertfordshire?

She sat down heavily on the trunk and wept bitterly for what might have been.